JARMAN, J.

The Crow Haunting

Sec. Fiction

Junior

For Dawn

I would like to thank Maureen, Stacy, Josh, Jo,
Becky and the B.D.A. for their help,
also the Archaeology Department of
Bedfordshire County Council.

Also by Julia Jarman
The Time Travelling Cat

The Crow Haunting was first published in Great Britain
by Andersen Press in 1996
Published in paperback by Collins in 1998
Collins is an imprint of HarperCollins*Publishers* Ltd
77-85 Fulham Palace Road, Hammersmith, London, W6 8JB

1 3 5 7 9 8 6 4 2

Text copyright © Julia Jarman 1996

ISBN 0 00 675213 6

The author asserts the moral right
to be identified as the author of the work.

Printed and bound in Great Britain by
Clays Ltd, St Ives plc

Chapter 1

They stood in front of the glass doors, Medi with the KwikMart trolley, wanting to step inside, and Davey her small brother pulling on her arm. He was protesting, she knew that, though he was saying he just wanted to watch the man with the trolleys. He wanted to see the man push the long trolley-snake from the car park to the trolley-park. It was in front of the revolving doors, but he didn't like the doors – that was the real trouble.

Sunrays bounced off the glass, splintering their reflections – of a tall girl, with long black hair curtaining her face, and two small boys. Joe-boy was crouching in the trolley pretending to be a lion, and he looked a bit like a lion with his golden hair. Davey was fair too, but not at all like Joe-boy in character. It was a hot day, the tarmac shimmered and Joe-boy roared. He was four. Davey was eight. Medi tried not to snap at Davey, but she wanted to get on with the shopping.

Cars crawled round the crowded car park – it was eleven o'clock on a Sunday – and exhaust fumes hung in the air.

The trolley-snake glistened and rattled.

'There, he's finished.'

'He hasn't. He's got to take its chain off.' Davey dragged on her arm.

'He's taken its chain off. Now come *on*!'

'Medi, look.' He was pointing at a line of crows – or rooks, large black birds anyway – standing in front of a yellow van. The van driver looked as if he was going to flatten them, but they flapped into the air at the last moment. Then they dangled like puppets before his windscreen.

'Come on, Davey.'

The birds lifted their feet and soared.

'Come *on*.'

He didn't move. 'That one's watching us, Medi.' He nodded towards the roof where a large crow was peering down at them. It looked like an old man, a judge with a black cape and a cap.

'We've got to do the shopping.' She felt uncomfortable. There were people behind them wanting to get in. She made room for them to pass. A lady with white hair and a suntanned face said, 'Don't worry about it, dear,' as she passed in a cloud of perfume.

Medi tried bribery. 'You can choose something nice.'

'Can I have a go on the spaceship?'

It was outside the doors, a ride-on which cost 20p. There was a giraffe too.

'When we've done the shopping.' The old man crow was still there, staring at them.

'Me too, Medi.' Joe-boy – he insisted on Joe-boy to distinguish himself from Jo-girl up the road – stopped being a lion and stood up. Bagga trailed from his hand. Bagga had been a bright yellow baby-gro. Now it was Joe-boy's comforter.

'You shouldn't have brought that old thing.' It was

grey and smelly.

'Bagga wants a ride on the spaceship.'

'Okay. But after the shopping.'

She'd have to shop carefully to be sure of having 40p to spare. Davey's hand gripped hers as they stepped into the doors. Why was he so scared of them? They stopped sometimes, but it wasn't dark inside, so they didn't close you in – not like in a lift – well, not usually. Was it the hissing sound of the brushes edging the doors? Or their own reflections on the steel surround? The shiny surface distorted things. She couldn't resist looking at her own reflection – it was her secret vice, looking in mirrors – and saw herself looking like a big fat crow! It made her laugh. She was wearing a black top with fringes on the cuffs, a bargain from Oxfam.

Davey's grip tightened. Oh no! The doors had stopped, trapping them inside. She thought fast before he panicked and made a scene.

'Davey! Look!' She pointed to the lights in the steel ceiling, which looked bright, futuristic even. 'Doesn't it look like a time-machine! Where do you want to go?' She talked rapidly though the doors were working again. 'Ancient Egypt? Roman Britain? Close your eyes and when you open them we'll be there!' Davey was into Romans – a Roman soldier had visited his school, an actor of course, claiming to be a time-traveller.

'Dinosaurland!' shouted Joe-boy. He was into dinosaurs – and guns.

Now the doors spilled them into the shop.

'Bang! Bang!' Joe-boy pointed two fingers. Why did

he want to shoot everything?

Medi ruffled Davey's hair. His eyes were still scrunched shut.

'You can open them now. Look, we've gone backwards in time! It says so.'

The cardboard façade of a Dickensian sweet shop stood just inside the doors, advertising Real Old-Fashioned Humbugs.

Davey read it aloud, and Joe-boy laughed. 'I'm a little humbug. Granny Smart says so.' A costumed lady gave them a stripy sweet each and Medi consulted her scribbled list.

Then they headed for the fruit and veg, the trolley a battleship now, cutting through the sea of shoppers. She was good at making a game of things.

'You're manning the periscope, Joe-boy. Tell us if you see danger.'

Later they played Burglar Bill.

'That's a nice tube of toothpaste with blue stripes on it!'

'We'll 'ave that!'

'That's a nice tin of beans with a Special Offer on it that's cheaper than the other kind.'

'We'll 'ave that!' the boys yelled, and people looked at them, but it was better than their asking for things they couldn't have, or moaning because they were bored. Fortunately there were dinosaurs on lots of things – and a free brontosaurus with the cornflakes they were going to buy anyway – so Joe-boy was happy.

The hardest bit was adding up as they went along, and

she was nervous that she wouldn't have enough money at the checkout, but she needn't have worried. She had enough and 40p over!

'The spaceship! The spaceship now!' yelled Joe-boy. They could see it through the glass windows fronting the store.

Davey looked pleased too. She packed the bags as quickly as she could, wanting to get through the doors before he started to worry again. But when they got to the exit, there was a crowd. The doors had stopped again, blocking the way out.

'Push them,' someone said.

'No, that's what stops them,' said someone else. 'It says "Don't push except in an emergency."'

Then a supervisor in a red coat said she was sorry but something had gone wrong, a power cut probably. The tills had stopped and the lights had gone out. For a second everything went quiet as people checked to see, and Medi looked round for something to take Davey's mind off the doors. She noticed a display of photographs, on the back wall, near the coffee shop, and led the boys over to it.

'Are we going to have a drink, Medi?'

'Sorry, Joe-boy. We haven't got enough money. Look at this instead.'

'Secrets of the Past.' Davey read out the display title proudly. Reading was something he could do and Joe-boy couldn't. Medi pointed to a photograph of a circle which looked a bit like Stonehenge.

She read out, *'Excavation of Neolithic Site,*

undertaken by East Hants Planning Department before construction of the superstore.'

'What does that mean, Medi?' Davey liked to know things.

'That they found a Stone Age settlement under the ground when they started to build this store. Stone Age people must have lived here. Look at that pot. It's almost as big as you.'

'Is it made of stone?'

'No, I don't think so.' It was an urn, *a collared urn*, made of clay, the caption said, *used for burying human remains*, but she didn't read that bit out. It would give Davey nightmares. There was a drawing of a girl pouring human ashes into the pot, using an animal's shoulder blade as a shovel.

'I thought they made everything out of stone. The Flintstones did.' Joe-boy loved the Flintstones.

'That's made of stone.' Davey was pointing to the photo of an enormous stone, used for grinding corn – a *quern*, the caption said – and another drawing of a young woman who might have used it. She had long hair and a dress which looked as if it had been made out of a sack, the hessian sort, not a plastic one.

'I thought they wore tiger skins,' said Joe-boy. 'Or bear skins. Or mammoth skins.'

Davey was interested in the Woodhenge.

'Read what it says, Medi.'

'Directly underneath this store was a circular ritual enclosure made over four thousand years ago. It was o' ⸳t 25 metres across and defined by a ditch. This

surrounded a ring of double wooden posts or totem poles.'

'Totem poles! Like Indians have?' asked Joe-boy. 'Bang! Bang!'

'Quiet, Joe-boy. Yes.'

'Did they have bows and arrows too?'

'I don't know.'

Davey said, 'Twenty-five metres, that's as wide as a football pitch.'

'Yes.' *Directly underneath them.* Medi saw the henge clearly in her mind's eye. She saw it at night-time lit by bonfires with people weaving in and out of the totem poles – dancing to the beat of drums. She could *hear* the drums. She could *feel* the throbbing beat beneath her feet!

'They're going again.' A voice brought her back to the present.

'The doors are working now. The electricity's back on.'

That's what she must have heard, the sound of the generators.

'Slowly! No more than one trolley per section!' The supervisor tried to control the surge of shoppers. 'Don't push! Can't you read?'

The doors stopped then started again as everyone tried to get through at once.

There was no point in hurrying and neither of the boys was eager to go.

They were fascinated by the pictures on the wall, Davey especially. He was reading all the captions beneath them. Joe-boy was shooting at something with the plastic brontosaurus.

'Look, Medi, skeletons! Bang! Bang!'

He was right. There was a photograph of two skeletons facing one another. A double burial it said, of two children, found in the top of the mound near the centre of the henge. *'Curled close together, they bear witness to a human tragedy four thousand years ago.'*

Reading it, Medi felt herself go cold. And she found herself wondering where exactly the two children had been buried. She could be walking over their grave. A shiver went through her.

'Somebody walking over your grave, dear?' A woman with straight white hair and a suntanned face stood beside her. She looked familiar, though for a moment Medi couldn't think why.

'What happened, Medi?' Davey was white. He'd read the description too. 'What happened to those children?'

'I don't know. I don't know everything you know.'

They both thought she did.

'How about that ride now?' She took hold of their hands as best she could with so many bags to carry. Then she drew them towards the doors, which stood still and empty now.

The white-haired woman followed them, still chatting – though Medi hadn't answered her first question – and they all stepped into the doors together.

'They go the wrong way, don't they?' The woman directed her talk to the boys now. 'That's why they keep stopping. They go widdershins.'

'Widdershins!' Joe-boy laughed at the word.

'They should go the other way like the sun and the moon.' The woman shook her head and her earrings spun. One was a silver moon and the other a bright yellow sun.

The doors went round slowly.

Keen to get out, Medi glanced through the glass to see if the spaceship was free, and she caught sight of a girl on the other side. For a second she thought it was her reflection, their reflection, for the girl held the hands of two smaller children. But the girl was shorter and plumper than Medi. She had long black hair, but it was plaited, and she wasn't dressed the same. She wore brown clothes which looked as if they were made of leather. Medi stared and their eyes met.

Then the girl *thinned out* as Medi watched her, and so did the two boys. Why was she so sure they were boys? They'd all been solid and then they had *thinned out*, become brown like an old photograph. Now they were just a shimmer like a heat haze.

What had she seen?

Even the shimmer had gone now.

'Come on, Medi.' Joe-boy was tugging at her sleeve, but she couldn't move.

Then she forced herself to move, forced herself to act normally.

She mustn't scare the boys.

'Come on, Davey.' Grabbing his hand, she led him into the sunlight.

'Out of the time-machine!' Joe-boy ran on towards

the ride-ons.

'Keep hold of my hand!' she yelled, but he was clambering onto the spaceship.

'You mustn't run off,' she gasped seconds later, propping the bags against the wall, and Joe-boy laughed and demanded 20p.

And Medi felt a rush of love for her brothers. She wanted to hold them close, and never let them out of her sight.

Chapter 2

They were so different – in character not looks – that's what made it so hard looking after them. One so fearless, the other so fearful. Point out danger and Davey's eyes grew large like a rabbit's. Not point it out and Joe-boy would talk to strangers as if they were old friends. And Davey was diabetic. That complicated matters. He had to have injections twice a day. He did them himself – with a Novopen. It was like a biro with a sharp point. He was ever so brave about that, but she had to make sure he remembered. Their mother said needles made her feel sick.

Who were those people?

She gave Joe-boy the 20p – Davey said he would wait for his ride, he was too old for the giraffe – and Medi thought how nice he was. Sometimes he seemed too good to be true. Joe-boy would have gone bananas if Davey had gone first. She glanced at her watch – it was twelve o'clock – and wondered whether they'd be home by twelve thirty. Davey had to eat at regular intervals. It was dangerous if he skipped meals. Perhaps he should have a snack now? What had they got that he could eat? Suddenly all her worries crowded in on her, boys to look after, homework waiting to be done. She'd been about to begin it when her mother had asked her to take the boys out. She could have done without the shopping trip, let alone seeing...

What? What had she seen?

'Just for an hour, Medi, while I give the house a going-through,' her mum had said.

It had taken over an hour already.

The old men crows were parading up and down the car park, and Davey was watching them. He must have seen those strange people. Why hadn't he said anything? Now he seemed to be talking to himself.

'What is it, Davey?'

He seemed miles away. Then he said, 'Who killed cock robin, Medi?

'"I," said the crow, "with my little bow."'

He laughed. 'I think it was that one, Medi.'

The old man crow was still peering down at them from the roof. The same crow? Surely not?

The spaceship stopped and she went to lift Joe-boy off, but he clung on.

'No! Me! More!'

Davey said, 'I don't mind, Medi, honest...'

But she insisted he had his turn. It wasn't good for Joe-boy to have his own way all the time.

Davey said, 'We could go on together if there's room.' And Joe-boy was delighted with his offer. Medi lifted Davey up. Joe-boy let him put the coin in and the machine began to rock. Up and down. To and fro. Joe-boy shrieked with happiness and Davey smiled, his arms round his little brother – and Medi felt herself going cold again. *Curled close together, they bear witness to a human tragedy four thousand years ago.* The words filled her head, turned her stomach to a hard ball. Suddenly she wished she had enough 20ps to let them ride for ever, for the world seemed full of danger.

There were more warnings all around her!

Behind them on the superstore windows – DANGER UNSEEN GERMS!

On a newspaper billboard near the door – CITY CENTRE CHILD SNATCH!

Beside a hole in the middle of the car park – DANGER ROAD UP!

And over at the filling station there was another – DANGER! INFLAMMABLE FUMES! DANGER! DANGER! DANGER! It was everywhere she looked!

'What's s-n-a-t-ch?' The spaceship had stopped. Davey was sounding out the newspaper headline.

'This!' She swung him into the air and down onto the paving stones.

'Me! Me! Joe-boy now!'

She swung him down too. Then they insisted on carrying a bag between them to help her, and set off while she was still picking the rest up.

'Stay near me! *Wait!*'

And they did wait – on the edge of the road that bordered the car park – with cars rushing by them. Though they weren't rushing, she could see that, but she also saw them skidding and swerving, mounting the pavement, crushing people. It was her imagination – she knew that – but it did happen, could happen. You heard about it. Again she wanted to hold the boys in her arms and swaddle them in love.

Then she remembered how sometimes she didn't even want to look after them, how she longed to say no when her mother asked her yet again – and guilt made her feel sick. Sarah, her best friend, as far as she had a best friend – there wasn't much time for friendship – Sarah said Medi should stand up to her mother. Sarah said Medi was Sacrificing her Youth for her mother's social life. Sarah's best subject was drama! She hadn't got a clue.

Holding the boys' hands while they crossed the road, Medi tried to calm down. She remembered other times she'd had feelings like this, premonitions that something terrible was going to happen. That their mother would leave them. That she'd never see her dad again. That she herself had an incurable disease and only months to live.

So far nothing that bad had happened. So far. She tried to cheer up.

The boys walked ahead of her, playing 'Beware of the Bears', trying to make each other stand on the lines of the street, or rather the pavement. It was quite wide and there wasn't much traffic – not dangerous at all. She caught them up and roared like a bear and Joe-boy shrieked with laughter. But she held their hands when they came to the roundabout and crossed the road to Oldbridge Road – the traffic was heavier here; it bordered an industrial estate.

Why had she seen those people?

She couldn't keep them out of her mind.

'Let's go that way, Medi.' Joe-boy was pointing to Bury Walk on the other side of the roundabout. It looked as if it was a short cut home, but it was a dead end. She'd tried it once. Dead end. Bury your dead. Was that why it was called Bury Walk? Were there bodies beneath the ground – skeletons and ashes in collared urns? Had that settlement extended as far as this?

She said, 'No, this way. That doesn't go anywhere. Keep near the hedge.' Because there weren't any short cuts to the Summer Meadows Estate where they lived. Unfortunately you had to walk right round the industrial estate to get to it. That meant following the Oldbridge Road, either on the far side which was lined with factories and warehouses, or on this side where there were fields. Beyond the hedge, on their right-hand side, it was farmland still – just as it had been four thousand years ago.

It wasn't hard to imagine those people living there, growing wheat and barley or something like it. Grinding it into flour with those enormous stones. She pictured the girl she'd seen heaving that heavy stone to and fro. Or perhaps she'd helped look after the sheep and cows? Did they look like the ones they were passing now? There were black cows and grey sheep in the field together. The farm house, Bury Farm, was further along, at the end of a long drive, hidden by trees.

Pausing to adjust the bags – fingers throbbing where they'd cut into her hands – Medi glanced back at the superstore, and saw in her mind's eye the mound and the Woodhenge crowning it. It must have been visible for miles around. She imagined people coming to it. Why? What had they used it for?

'No!' A shout – from Davey – brought her back to the present. He was trying to stop Joe-boy from crossing the road to Futurama Computers where their mother worked on weekdays.

'Joe! NO!' She shouted too and caught them up a few seconds later. Then they crossed the road together. The turning to Ouse Road was just ahead of them. Ouse Road led eventually to Poppy Gardens where they lived.

Davey was looking a bit pale, but when she asked him how he was feeling, he said he was okay. She promised a snack as soon as they got in and Joe-boy said, 'Me too, Medi. I want a snack.' Then they reached the board saying SUMMER MEADOWS WELCOMES CARE-FUL DRIVERS. This was their cue for take-off – now they could reach their door without crossing any roads – so they took off.

As she watched them running past the Michelin factory, arms outstretched, and then past the cemetery on the other side, Medi thought about Sarah again. Spooky, that's what Sarah called it, living near a cemetery but it didn't look spooky at all. It was more like a park really – the gardens were full of roses – and the buildings in the middle, the chapel and the crematorium, weren't too different from the KwikMart they'd just been to. The chapel had a clock tower and so did the KwikMart. They were both built of red brick. No, it didn't look spooky at all, but today as she passed, it reminded her of what she'd seen earlier. Those people had cremated some bodies and buried others – just like us.

Ghosts. There, she'd said it. Thought it anyway. She

thought of the girl and longed to know more about her. Maybe there was something she could read?

Then, a passing car reminded her of Davey and Joe-boy. Where were they? For a moment she couldn't see them. Panic. Then she spotted them – on the corner of Poppy Gardens – and she was running.

She caught them up outside 5 Poppy Gardens.

'Next house, boys!'

'I know the way, Medi.'

'I know the way too, Medi. My name is Joe-boy Simmonds. I live at 3 Poppy Gardens, Summer Meadows, East Hampton.' Oh dear, she'd offended both of them.

The boys' surname was Simmonds because Medi's mother had married their father after she'd divorced Medi's. Medi had kept her dad's surname, Bonnard.

'Who taught you that?' She tried to nudge Joe-boy with her knee – because her hands were full – and jolly him out of his bad mood. She'd taught both of them their names and their addresses, in case they ever got lost.

But Joe-boy wouldn't be jollied. He was stomping up the path now, and their mother was opening the door. Fair like Joe-boy, her hair tied back with a ribbon, Jenny Simmonds – she liked Medi to call her Jenny – looked girlish. She was younger than Medi's friends' mothers – and she looked it. Sometimes Medi felt older than her mother.

'I wanted to ring the bell.' Joe-boy was protesting.

'Sorry, Joe.' She ruffled his hair and tried to hug him.

'Joe-boy.' He glared at her.

'Sorry, Joe-boy. Hello, Davey. Why aren't you helping Medi with the bags?'

'They did, both of them, most of the way. They've been good really.'

The boys disappeared upstairs and Medi, adjusting the shopping bags, saw that her fingers were blue. No wonder they hurt. Jenny rattled the door handle.

'Come on, Medi, don't stand there dreaming. Get inside before the frozen stuff melts.'

As Medi stepped inside, a peal of laughter made her look up – at Davey leaning out of his bedroom window! Joe-boy too!

'Get back inside!'

'The wolf, Medi, he's behind you!'

'Don't be silly!' She tried to keep the panic out of her voice. It was Davey's newest joke. There was a board for Wolfe Manufacturing on the other side of the road. 'Get back inside! You'll fall out!' She waited for them to obey her. Where was her mum when the boys needed telling?

As she closed the front door both boys appeared at the top of the stairs.

'Got you, Medi! Got you!'

Her mother was in the kitchen which looked no tidier than when she'd left it, but she had made some sandwiches for lunch. Jenny and the boys ate theirs while Medi put the shopping away. Jenny said she was a treasure and she didn't know what she would do without her, she really didn't.

Later, when they were having a cup of tea in the

sitting room, Medi wondered about telling what she'd seen in KwikMart, but she couldn't think how to begin and she didn't know how Jenny would react. She'd probably giggle and then get on the phone to her friend Eileen. And there was something else on her mind. Her mum hadn't done much cleaning.

'Who's been?'

'No one. Why?'

'The room smells different.'

'You and your nose, Medi.' Jenny laughed. Medi's 'nose' was notorious, but not entirely a laughing matter. If it hadn't been for her sense of smell Davey's diabetes might not have been diag-*nosed* before it was too late. At first Jenny had laughed when Medi said Davey smelt sugary. His breath had smelt like nail varnish remover. Then she'd taken him to the doctor. This smell was different though.

Jenny said, 'It's polish. I've been cleaning remember.'

But the smell reminded Medi of someone.

'Has my dad been?' She hadn't seen him for ages. He worked on oil rigs in the North Sea. The smell was a bit like his aftershave.

'No, Medi.'

'Caveman, then?' That was their joke-name for Des, the boys' dad. That marriage hadn't worked out either. Once, when Medi had asked, Jenny had said that Frank – that was Medi's dad – had been too soft and that Des, the boys' dad, had been too hard. Medi couldn't help thinking of Goldilocks.

'Who has been then?' A new boyfriend perhaps? One

that was just right?

'I've told you. No one, Medi!' Jenny looked Medi in the eye, but she emptied her cup quickly and walked into the kitchen.

Medi went upstairs to start her homework. On the way to her room she looked in on the boys. They'd built themselves a pirate ship out of Lego. The pirates had lost their daddy, they said, but they were going to find him. Poor things. She thought about her own dad and how much she missed him, but at least he wrote to her from time to time. Then she wished, as she often did, that her mother could see her dad's good points. They'd been happy once. She had a photograph which proved it. It was on her dressing table – Frank and Jenny, and herself as a baby all face and feet facing the camera. When had they changed from that to this? When had she changed? She glanced at herself in the winged mirror and examined the three Medis staring back at her. She liked the right-hand one best. You did change suddenly, in jumps, not gradually. Once she'd grown a whole shoe-size in one day.

Frank still loved Jenny – that's what he told Medi anyway. But it was no good dreaming about that sort of happy ending, it was strictly fiction. She picked up *A Midsummer Night's Dream*. Or perhaps not. Even Shakespeare seemed to think love was a here-today-gone-tomorrow sort of feeling. That, funnily enough, was what she had to write about – the different sorts of love in *A Midsummer Night's Dream*. Well, it was more interesting than shopping for toothpaste. She got stuck in.

When Jenny's shouts interrupted her thoughts, it seemed like only minutes later.

'Medi! Did you see any of this? Come here!'

'What? I'm doing my homework.'

'You've been at it for hours. Listen to this!'

Her mother was watching the local news where a reporter was saying that New Age travellers had been causing trouble all over the country. Convoys of them were converging on sites like Stonehenge to celebrate the summer solstice, and one convoy had arrived in East Hampton. Some of the travellers had been seen in KwikMart. Midsummer was only two days away.

'It seems there used to be a sort of Stonehenge where the store is now,' said Jenny.

'I know,' said Medi, only half listening because the woman she'd seen in KwikMart was on the screen, the one with white hair and the sun and moon earrings.

Now Jenny was laughing. 'It's that Mrs Whatsit with a foreign sounding name. Listen to her.'

'I'm trying to,' said Medi. The woman – a Mrs Vogel – was saying the people seen in KwikMart weren't New Age travellers. They were time-travellers – ghosts from prehistoric times. That's what ghosts were. She'd seen them.

'Bit of a fruitcake if you ask me,' laughed Jenny. 'Eileen went to her Circle of Light to have her fortune told. Wasn't she one of those protesters, who didn't want the store to be built? Doesn't stop her using it though.

21

I've seen her in there. Did you see her today?'

Medi didn't answer. She didn't know what to say. She thought about finding Davey and asking him if he'd seen anything odd in KwikMart, but she didn't want to put ideas in his head if he hadn't.

That night though, he had a bad dream which woke him up – and it woke Medi. He was yelling, 'I don't want to go! I don't want to go!' It took her quite a while to calm him down and even longer to get him back to sleep.

But in the morning he had no memory of it.

Chapter 3

Medi longed to talk to someone about what she had seen, and next morning as she pulled on her ghastly green uniform, she though she might mention it to Sarah at school. But even before she reached Towers High, actually a cluster of concrete blocks, she'd decided against it. It was obvious from snatches of conversation overheard on the way, and the howled greetings, that the KwikMart ghosts were the biggest laugh since Rory Mcgrew had tied the Head's pyjamas to St Oswald's steeple on April Fools' Day. Well, he always said they were the Head's pyjamas.

Sarah, when Medi met her by the school bottle bank, was full of it all. She'd seen the news item and she'd just been talking to Harvey Bremner who stacked shelves at KwikMart in the evenings. She said that he said that quite a few weird things had happened there, though he'd never seen anything himself, but several people said they'd heard drumming *and* chanting *and* high-pitched cries coming from beneath the floor, and a few said they'd seen strange looking people near the doors which often broke down. One of the checkout staff had actually left, convinced that a ghost had thrown a packet of crisps at her!

Sarah loved the drama of it all, it was obvious, and she'd have loved it even more if Medi had added her bit, and that perversely was what stopped Medi telling her. Sarah would have been too interested, too enthusiastic – and she'd have told the rest of the school. When both local papers ran the story, she was glad she hadn't said anything. It was bad enough reading about the Superstore Spooks without seeing her own name in print. She'd have liked to have talked to Harvey Bremner though.

It was typical, that he lived a couple of doors away from Medi, at 7 Poppy Gardens, and that Sarah had had a whole jokey conversation with him, while Medi was hardly on hello terms. When they'd first moved in, Jenny had invited his mother round for coffee, but his mother hadn't invited Jenny back. Sarah said she'd said, 'Where does all this spooky stuff happen then, in the spirits' department?' and he'd laughed at her joke. Sarah said she thought Harvey was good-looking, like a blond cavalier, and when she came round the following Monday, Medi couldn't help wondering who she'd really come to see.

Jenny, having one of her rare nights at home, let Sarah in. She liked Sarah, who'd had her red hair done in a new spiky style. She said she'd come to ask Medi to go to a film with her – on Wednesday. It was called 'The Crow', and she read out a review, in a dramatically spooky voice which made Jenny laugh. '"*If somebody dies before their time a crow visits their grave and allows them to repay their debts. If the crow is injured, however, then the person begins to feel pain; and if it is killed then the spirit of the person dies with it. Thus* begins one of the most talked about films of the year.'"

Jenny said it sounded fun – but that unfortunately Medi couldn't go, because she'd have to look after the boys every night that week, as she, Jenny, was working the twilight shift at Futurama. Monday was her only night at home.

As it happened Medi didn't like the sound of the film anyway, though the subject matter intrigued her. Obviously she and Davey weren't the only ones to find crows scary. She read the review again after Sarah had gone. It was in the local paper with a picture of a crow in a graveyard, looking just like the one in the KwikMart car park. No, she didn't fancy that at all.

She thought of going to see the weird Mrs Vogel, but didn't, and then she came across her in KwikMart about three weeks later. She didn't look weird at all, but quite nice really. At first they – Davey and Joe-boy were with her – saw her through the glass. She was just inside the doors choosing flowers. Davey was very quiet and Medi thought he was going to refuse to go in, but he didn't even try the usual stalling activities. He just held her hand very tightly when the doors went round. Fortunately they didn't break down.

As they passed Mrs Vogel, Joe-boy said, 'There's the widdershins lady!' and she looked up and laughed. She was wearing a top with a shiny unicorn on it, and Joe-boy said, 'That's a nice horse,' and Mrs Vogel looked as if she was going to say something, but Medi hurried on to the fruit and veg. But when they were at the checkout, Mrs Vogel came to the same one.

25

Medi found herself handing her the NEXT CUSTOMER thing, when Davey said he needed the toilet. It was a bit worrying – only seconds before he'd been asking for a drink – and she thought he ought perhaps to check his blood-sugar level – but she hadn't packed all their shopping yet. It was awkward and she was wondering what to do when Mrs Vogel said she'd watch Joe-boy and their things while Medi took Davey to the loo if she wanted. Davey said he was desperate, so she accepted.

Davey did just need the loo. He had got his testing kit – and she insisted he did a blood test – but fortunately everything was fine. When they came out he said he wanted to look at the pictures of the excavation, so she left him looking at the display on the wall while she collected Joe-boy and the shopping from Mrs Vogel. Then they all found themselves looking at the display, and Mrs Vogel was saying it was a crying shame to have destroyed something magical like that. She emphasised the word magical and Medi didn't know what to say, so she mumbled something about finding it fascinating. There were questions she was dying to ask, but not while Davey was listening. Then Mrs Vogel said that if Medi was fascinated she ought to come along to the circle, the Circle of Light. It was a group of ladies, well ladies mostly, there was one gentleman, who met at her house to explore such mysteries. Or, if Medi preferred a different approach, because the circle wasn't everyone's cup of tea, then she should go to the library. There were articles about the site in a magazine called *East Hamptonshire Archaeology*. She could read it in the Local History section.

Walking home, Medi wished she had managed to ask Mrs Vogel about the people they'd both seen. Were they one of the mysteries the Circle of Light explored? Did Mrs Vogel think the boys they'd seen on the other side of the doors were the same boys who had been buried on the mound? Did she think they were a warning? Did she think there was some connection with Medi's brothers? Did she think they were in danger? There were loads of questions she was dying to ask. She didn't like the sound of the Circle of Light though. Weirdos, her mother had called them, and she was probably right.

Besides, it was nearly a month since she'd seen the figures, and the boys were okay – touch wood. She touched a hazel twig in the hedge beside the Oldbridge Road.

Maybe she was worrying unnecessarily. There was no harm in doing a bit of research though, so she'd go to the library as soon as she could.

That was the following Monday after school. Local History was upstairs on a balcony overlooking the children's section, so she was able to leave the boys there. Davey wanted to come up with her, but she told him he had to look after Joe-boy. She could see them both all the time, even when she was asking the librarian for help. The librarian, a friendly lady whose glasses

27

made her look like an owl, tapped the keys of a computer for a few minutes, then fetched a copy of *East Hamptonshire Archaeology*.

The article didn't tell Medi much more than she already knew. It said that eleven people in all were buried in the henge which had been used as a ritual site in the Stone Age, and it said that two children had been buried in a single grave with a separate burial of a young adult nearby. She copied it all down, and even made sketches of the enormous pot and the quern used for grinding corn. But when the librarian said, 'Was that helpful, dear?' she said, 'I really wanted to know how the children died.'

The librarian thought a bit, then said it might be worth going to the museum. Some of the finds might be on show there.

They went the next day. Unfortunately she had to take the boys, though she would like to have checked it out first. It probably wasn't a good idea to let Davey see the skeletons. But she needn't have worried. They weren't on show. When Medi asked about the prehistoric settlement, the man at reception directed them upstairs to the Prehistory section where there was quite a lot of stuff in glass cases, including a piece of mammoth's tusk and the tooth of a sabre-toothed tiger. Joe-boy was delighted! Mammoths and sabre-toothed tigers really had roamed over East Hamptonshire, and hippos had swum in the river! There were several stone axes that Stone Age man might have killed them with, and some flint arrows!

'So they did have bows and arrows, Medi!' He was ecstatic.

The mammoths and the tiger and the hippo belonged to the Old Stone Age, thousands of years before the henge at KwikMart had been built, but Joe-boy wasn't interested in these fine distinctions.

Davey looked at everything avidly and read all the captions.

There were a few pots from the New Stone Age, and Medi studied them. The people she had seen could have used pots like them. They were quite nice, better than the ones she'd made when she'd had a go at pottery! Archaeologists called the tribe which used them the Beaker people, because they'd found lots of beakers with quite intricate lined patterns on them, but there wasn't anything from the KwikMart site.

The man at the desk apologised. He said that the county council must still have the pots and skeletons and things. He gave Medi the number of the council's Archaeology department and suggested she ring them.

Medi rang when they got home and said she wanted to know about the children's skeletons on the Neolithic site under KwikMart. She wanted to know how the children had died.

Someone – Medi thought it was a woman though she had a deep voice – said she couldn't help much because they were still waiting for a pathologist's report. When Medi said she didn't understand, the woman said pathologists were experts at working out why people had died. They examined the bones for injuries and they did chemical tests on fragments, but the department couldn't afford one. They'd run out of money, so the skeletons had been catalogued and put into storage. They hadn't even got enough money to publish what they had found out.

Medi said, 'What did you find out? How do you think they died?'

The woman sounded a bit impatient, probably because it was nearly six o'clock and she wanted to get home. She said,'Your guess is as good as mine, dear. It could have been an accident. It could have been ritual murder.' She said she'd send Medi a leaflet they'd printed when they'd done the dig about five years ago, if she could find one. Now if Medi would give her her address.

Murder! And that word *ritual* again.

Later, when the boys were in bed, she looked it up in the dictionary.

> ritual *a & n l.a* Of, with, consisting in, involving
> religious or other rites; ritual murder, sacrifice of
> person to god(s).

Surely the boys weren't in danger of that! Though you did read of weird things in the papers. She looked up *murder* too:

> murder *n* Unlawful killing of human being with
> malice aforethought.

Well yes, she knew that. Something else caught her eye though,

> murder *n* collective noun for a group of crows; a
> murder of crows.

Weird.

When Sarah came round later on, she mentioned it to her, but Sarah had more exciting things to talk about, Harvey Bremner and his friend Gray Parker to be precise, who had invited her – and Medi if she liked – to go to KwikMart *with them* next day after school. Gray would show them where a ghost had thrown a packet of crisps at his auntie Kath. She was the one who'd worked on the checkout till she resigned.

'What do you think of that, Medi Bonnard? I know you've been longing to talk to your lovely neighbour!'

When she stopped giggling she said the crow film had been ace.

Chapter 4

Medi couldn't go to KwikMart with them, of course, and didn't know whether she wanted to. At half past three next day she was outside Ravenston Primary School, waiting for Davey to come out, and Joe-boy, whom she'd collected from the nursery, was hanging on her arm.

'Swing, Medi! *Swing*!'

Trying to distract him, she pointed to the raven, spinning on the spire of St Oswald's church next door. The raven was St Oswald's emblem – as Davey never tired of telling them. The spire was made of steel and looked a bit like a rocket. The raven looked like a jet fighter. School and church were both modern buildings, built mostly of glass and concrete.

Joe-boy said he'd like to climb to the top of the spire.

'He's a handful, that one,' said Jo-girl's mother as Jo-girl came skipping down the school steps, blonde curls bobbing. 'Not like his brother, is he?' Davey was just behind Jo-girl, walking carefully with the leaf he'd taken in that morning. Medi was pleased to see him looking happy. He'd been rather withdrawn lately. He'd found the leaf on a walk. It was like lace, the skeleton of a holly leaf. He smiled when he saw her and she gave him a hug – being careful not to crush the leaf – and so did Joe-boy.

She said, 'What did Mrs McNerney say?' Mrs McNerney was his class teacher.

'She said it was beautiful.'

'Did she show the other children?'

He nodded and said he'd had to take it round all the classes, so everyone could see it.

'I thought you were going to leave it at school on the talk-and-show table.'

He said he wanted to take it to Cubs with him. He'd get points for it then – for his pack.

Cubs night! She'd forgotten about that. They'd better get home. A vague idea she'd had, of going to Kwik-Mart with the boys was abandoned. There was too much to do. Cubs was at six o'clock in the Beechwood Lane Community Centre, which was further than KwikMart even. So back to Plan A – to call in on the way back with Joe-boy, by which time Sarah and friends would have gone. She had to call in because she'd made a bargain with Joe-boy to get him to be good. She'd promised him a ride on the spaceship – or some sweets – if he didn't make a scene when they left Davey at Cubs. He hated the long walk, all the way there and all the way back, and all the way back again, and he hated Davey going to Cubs without him.

At first she thought the bribe wasn't going to work. At six o'clock he was refusing to move. The Cubs, in a circle round Akela, were beginning to howl and Joe-boy looked as if he was going to howl too. 'It's not fair!'

She reminded him of their bargain. 'What are you

going to have, some sweets or a ride on the spaceship?'
'Both.'

She didn't say there wasn't enough money for both and when they got there both riding-toys were out of order – but Joe-boy seemed content to go inside and choose some sweets. So far so good. She felt a bit daft with a trolley, which Joe-boy insisted on, with only 25p to spend, but she didn't see anyone she knew. If Harvey Bremner was stacking shelves he was doing it in another section.

Joe-boy took so long to choose – though he eventually narrowed the choice to Blu-its which made your mouth blue and Boneshakers which were bone-shaped – that she began to think they might be able to spin out the time and not go back home before fetching Davey, but he suddenly decided on the Boneshakers – in a red plastic coffin – and demanded to be taken into the time-machine.

'Right, where do you want to go?' she said when they stood inside the doors.

'Dinosaurland!' he shouted. 'Close your eyes, Medi!'

He enjoyed it so much – how different from Davey he was – that they went round several times and it was only when she got bored that she remembered the strange sight she'd seen weeks earlier. It made her put her arm round Joe-boy who shrugged it off. 'Close your eyes, Medi!'

Shuffling forwards, she closed then opened them, and found herself facing the car park looking straight at Harvey Bremner – who loped past – and Mrs Vogel, who laughed.

Face burning, Medi steered Joe-boy out of the way, but Mrs Vogel was her usual chatty self. All a-glitter in earrings and a shimmery top, she addressed Joe-boy first. 'Where's your brother today?' But Joe-boy was too interested in his Boneshakers to answer. Medi, wishing she wasn't so polite, answered for him. Then Mrs Vogel asked if the Cubs Davey went to were in Beechwood Lane, and when Medi nodded, she launched into a spiel about going there herself a few weeks earlier.

'Didn't Davey say so? I took some of my animals to show the boys. Some of them were doing their Animal Care badge. I think I remember seeing Davey.'

Now Joe-boy was listening, and Medi could see his mind working. Had Davey seen something he hadn't?

'What animals?' He frowned at her.

'Well, at the moment I've got a swan with one wing, a family of hedgehogs and a seagull and a donkey. I look after them you see, if they're injured. Till they get better. Wild Life Rescue, that's me. You may have seen me in the papers.'

Medi said, 'I think Davey would have said, if he'd seen the animals, Joe-boy.' She wanted to get going.

But Mrs Vogel was saying, 'Would *you* like to see my animals, Joe-boy?' She looked at her watch and turned to Medi. 'It's twenty to seven. What time do you meet Davey? Half past is it? Well, if we go to my house now, you can see all my furry and feathered friends and then collect him. It will save you going home.'

'*Please*, Medi.' Joe-boy smiled sweetly.

'It's not far.' Mrs Vogel waved in the direction of the Oldbridge Road.

Medi knew Jenny would not like them to go so she said she didn't think there was time, but Mrs Vogel said they could go straightaway. She'd been to the bottle bank, and she hadn't got any shopping to do. And she didn't live far away. In fact they'd passed her house lots of times. It was opposite Futurama Computers. She'd watched them go by lots of times. That didn't make Medi feel better.

'Cwark,' said an old man crow by her foot.

'Please, Medi.' Joe-boy gave her his blond-angel look. He'd have caused a riot if she'd said no.

'Come *on*,' said Mrs Vogel.

With a feeling of unease Medi watched Joe-boy talking non-stop to Mrs Vogel as they walked back to her house. He showed her his Boneshakers and she shuddered as if they were real bones, and he explained that they were really only sherbety sweets and she said, 'Really?' as if she didn't know and he gave her one.

Her house was a cottage called Wychwood – there was a sign on the gate – and Medi thought it was odd that she'd never noticed it before. It was in a bit of a hollow – you went down a path to get to it – and there was a hedge in front of it, but it wasn't exactly hidden. When they got to the gate Mrs Vogel said Wychwood was a reference to the wych elms which used to grow here and didn't mean she was a witch! Joe-boy laughed, but Medi couldn't. The walls were brown like biscuits and made her think of Hansel and Gretel.

Fortunately Mrs Vogel didn't invite them in. In fact she told them to wait outside the back door, while she fetched Gulliver the gull. While they waited Joe-boy tipped his sweets onto a small table and tried to make a skeleton out of them. Since they were mostly hands – Medi counted six at a glance – he said maybe it was two skeletons, then Mrs Vogel came out with Gulliver on her shoulder. He was a herring gull. The top of his head was black, and so were his feet. Someone had run over one of his feet in KwikMart car park. He was better now, but wouldn't leave her. Then she said they ought to hurry if they wanted to see her other furry and feathered friends.

Bottom, the donkey, in a field behind the cottage, was an immediate hit with Joe-boy. Mrs Vogel said he had been a seaside donkey – till he'd been turned loose with no one to look after him. Someone had found him wandering on a railway line and it was a miracle he hadn't been killed. Joe-boy asked if he could have a ride, and Mrs Vogel lifted him onto his back saying, 'You'll have to ride bareback, Joe-boy. Like an Indian. Medi will make sure you don't fall off. Go as far as the river and back.'

Then she left them – to go and make a cup of tea, she said.

Medi started to relax a bit. Joe-boy was blissfully happy – and Bottom seemed a very steady animal. All she had to do was walk by his side. It was a nice way of filling the time.

As she walked she wondered if Mrs Vogel had given Bottom his name, and whether she'd got the idea from *A*

Midsummer Night's Dream, and her mind wandered to her essay on love, which she hadn't got back yet, when a laugh from Joe-boy interrupted her thoughts. 'What was that you said?' Actually it was good she had looked up. They were nearly at the river.

'I said Bottom's got a big bottom like a . . .'

'Like a what?' She couldn't hear properly; there were a lot of noisy ducks in the reed beds.

'Like a *bottom of course!*' he yelled and the ducks flew into the air. Then she did have to hold him on, he was laughing so much. Fortunately the donkey stood still, staring into the water. There had been a lot of rain lately. The willows on the other side seemed to be wading in water. Further along KwikMart seemed to rise from the water as the Woodhenge must have done when the river flooded in prehistoric times.

Checking her watch – it was just gone seven – she started to turn the donkey round and saw Mrs Vogel walking towards them, with a swan by her side, a cygnet really. Its feathers were still grey and it staggered a bit.

'Meet Sinbad,' she said when they met in the middle of the field, 'Sinbad the sailor, get it? Because he rolls from side to side like an old sea-dog. Poor fellow, he's only got one wing, you see.' He'd flown into an electricity pylon, she said. His other wing had been a terrible mess. She'd had to take him to the vet's to have it removed.

'But he can swim beautifully. You'll see in a minute. Look.' So they turned towards the river again as Sinbad lurched towards it, gathering pace as he careered down

the slope. Then in a shower of glittering droplets he was
in the water, and he did swim beautifully. They watched
for several minutes. Then Mrs Vogel said, 'Come on or
he'll stay there for ever.' They set off for the house, and
after a bit he followed them.

There were three mugs of tea on the table outside the
back door. Sinbad sat with his head on Mrs Vogel's lap
while she drank hers.

The mugs had signs of the zodiac on them. 'What are
you?' she asked Medi.

'Virgo.'

'I guessed right! Isn't your name Welsh for
September?'

'Yes.' Not many people knew that.

'You're Welsh then?'

'Sort of.' My dad is. She didn't say that though, didn't
feel like explaining. Instead she looked at her watch. It
was just gone seven. *Just gone seven – still!* Oh no! Her
watch had stopped! 'W-what's the time?' she
stammered.

'Twenty-five past. Oh dear.'

They ran all the way there. Mrs Vogel said she was sorry
she hadn't noticed the time. She was sorry she didn't
have a car – or even a bike. She said Joe-boy could stay
with her, so that Medi could run faster, but Medi said he
couldn't. She didn't care if she sounded rude. Joe-boy
was amazingly good. Medi said they were running in the
Marathon. She said they were running in the Olympics.
She said they were breaking all the records – and it was

probably true.

But Davey wasn't there.

They were only five minutes late, but Akela was locking the door of the community centre. In her green uniform and glasses she looked like a bull frog.

Everyone had gone, she said. All the children had been collected.

'You didn't let him go by himself?'

'Of course not.' She said she would never let any boy go by himself.

'Then who . . . collected him?' Medi could hardly speak. She was engulfed by fear.

It couldn't have been their mother. She was still at work.

Akela said she must ask Bagheera who was putting things in the car.

She came back with another woman, Bagheera; her real name was Mrs Bentley; she was in the green uniform too. She said Davey's dad had collected him.

'His *dad*?'

'Yes. He came and told me his dad had come for him.'

'Did you see him? What did he look like?'

Mrs Bentley didn't answer and Medi knew she hadn't seen him.

It had happened.

Chapter 5

Akela – whose real name was Mrs Smithers – took them home in her car. She said she was sure Davey would be there with his daddy. Joe-boy said he was sure too. He sat on the back seat by Medi sucking Bagga. 'I'm going home to see my daddy. I'm going home to see my daddy.' He said it several times, taking Bagga out of his mouth so as to speak clearly, then stuffing it in again. Medi didn't say anything. She couldn't. She just looked out of the window – while Mrs Smithers prattled on. She said Davey was one of the best behaved little boys in Beechwood Pack. He was quiet but a joiner-in. He wouldn't do anything that wasn't sensible. She was sure he wouldn't. He was on his knots badge.

She drove quite fast talking all the time. Had their daddy got a car or would he be walking with Davey? Joe-boy said he thought his daddy had a big car, probably a Porsche, a red one.

There were several cars in Poppy Gardens, but none in front of Number 3. Medi was out of the car almost before Mrs Smithers had stopped it, and she'd opened the front door before Joe-boy had undone his seatbelt. She could hear him yelling, 'Wait for me!' as she turned the key.

'Davey! Des! Are you here?' Her voice sounded echoey. She knew the house was empty. From the hall, she could see the empty kitchen. It didn't take long to see that there was no one in the sitting room.

'Davey! Des!' She raced upstairs but nobody answered. There was no one in the bedrooms.

Then Joe-boy was by her side, at the top of the stairs.

'Where are they, Medi?' He took hold of her hand, and sucked hard on Bagga.

'They're not back yet then?' Mrs Smithers was at the bottom of the stairs, with her mouth open. 'Where's your mum, dear?'

'At work.' Thinking that the boys are safe with me – she didn't say. And Mrs Smithers said that Davey's dad could have taken him to the shop perhaps, to buy some sweets.

Joe-boy said, 'Let's go to the shop, Medi.'

But Medi said she was going to ring their mum, and she rang Futurama who said Mrs Simmonds wasn't there. She hadn't been in that day.

That was odd. What was going on? Jenny hadn't said anything about not going to work. But at least she must have met Davey. Perhaps her mum *and* Des had met him. Hope surged.

But Jenny came in minutes later – alone.

She didn't say where she'd been. She listened to Medi and Mrs Smithers, then she rang the police. Her voice shook. Medi heard her saying, 'M-my little boy – he's eight – has disappeared. He was last seen at the Cub meeting in Beechwood Community Centre. He may have gone off with a man.'

Medi said, 'Not a man, Mum. Des. Mrs Bentley said

Davey's dad.' Forcing herself to think rationally, she had come to the conclusion that Mrs Bentley was right. Des must have met Davey, and taken him back to his place – which wasn't as bad as what she originally feared.

But Jenny wasn't listening. She was telling Mrs Smithers to stay and she was asking for Mrs Bentley's address. The police wanted it, she said. She didn't say anything to Medi. She didn't look at her. It was as if she wasn't there.

Medi didn't blame her. What could she say? It's not your fault? She couldn't say that. It was her fault. She shouldn't have been late.

As soon as she'd put down the phone, Jenny picked it up again and rang round Davey's friends. None of them gave her the answer she wanted. She rang her best friend Eileen.

Then she started to tidy the kitchen – with quick efficient movements. Medi had never seen her like this. It was as if she thought that by putting everything in its place, she could make things right. She wouldn't sit down, wouldn't stop snapping doors shut and wiping surfaces. Wouldn't look at Medi, who tried again to speak to her.

'Why don't you ring Des? Where does he live?'

But Jenny didn't answer. She was re-arranging the cups in the cup cupboard now. Medi thought she wasn't answering because Mrs Smithers was still there. They could both see her, on the settee in the sitting room, with her head in her hands. But what did it matter if Mrs

Smithers heard? Why the secrecy? Lots of marriages broke down. It happened all the time. And this sort of thing happened – fathers wanting custody of their children. You read about it in the papers. Now this would be in the papers.

Des must have snatched Davey, taken him to live with him, which was bad but not as bad as other things she could think of. They could probably get Davey back.

She looked at her mother who was rubbing the clear surfaces now.

'Mum. Jenny . . .' But Jenny didn't even look up.

Then the doorbell rang and Medi ran to open it.

Two police officers, a man and a woman, introduced themselves as PC Watkins and WPC Donkin. Medi took them into the sitting room, where WPC Donkin tried to be reassuring. She said that in ninety-nine cases out of a hundred, the missing child turned up. They mustn't presume the worst, but they must take it seriously. There had been an incident like this a month before. Medi remembered the newspaper headline. CITY CENTRE CHILD SNATCH. They had found the child that time.

'Now,' said WPC Donkin, if they would all tell herself and PC Watkins as much as they could . . .

When they went, over an hour later with photos of Davey and pages of notes, they warned against despair again, but Medi thought they looked less hopeful. They said the police were already looking and they must all look on the bright side, but Mrs Smithers was crying as she left. She said she would never forgive herself, never, and Medi knew exactly how she felt.

Why couldn't *she* cry?

Why couldn't her mother? She was polishing the kettle now.

'Mum, why did you send me to the kitchen when PC Watkins asked about Dad?'

'To make some tea.'

'I mean really.'

She'd had to take Joe-boy with her, and Jenny had closed the door behind them.

Jenny didn't answer, but she was thinking, Medi could tell, stalling. The policeman had called her back in soon afterwards and asked if he could help with the tea. He'd listened politely when Medi had asked if the police were watching the ports and the airports, in case Des was trying to leave the country with Davey, but there was something in his expression which said he wasn't taking her seriously.

She'd had the feeling that he and her mother knew something she didn't. She still had that feeling.

'Mum, why did you send me out?'

'I didn't want Joe-boy to hear.'

'Hear what?'

'About his dad.'

'Hear what about his dad?'

'That he's gone, of course.'

'But Joe-boy knows he's gone. He's not daft. Nor am I! Joe-boy said he wished his dad had taken him too.'

'Des has *not* taken Davey!'

'How can you be so sure?'

'Don't interrogate me, Medi!'

Why couldn't she give a straight answer? Why the mystery?

When Medi put Joe-boy to bed he said, 'Davey will be here in the morning, won't he, Medi? That nice police lady will find him.'

Chapter 6

Medi and her mum didn't go to bed. Jenny wanted to stay near the phone. Medi didn't know what to do. She hated being by herself, but when she sat in the sitting room she could *feel* Jenny despising her. She was furious with Medi for going to Mrs Vogel's.

'She's weird, Medi. Why did she keep you so long? That's what I want to know.'

She said she'd told the police about her. She'd told them that they ought to keep an eye on people like that. She told them about the Circle of Light, about Eileen going to it once – to have her fortune told. Mrs Vogel had read the runes, whatever they were.

Had Mrs Vogel kept them? Had she made them late deliberately? Mightn't they have been even later if they'd gone all the way home? Question after question whirred in Medi's brain. She still thought there was a chance Des had taken Davey. It was the obvious explanation. Davey had said, 'My dad's here now.' Why would he say that if it wasn't true? On the other hand it was a long time since he'd seen his father. Two years or more. Could he have gone off with someone else pretending to be his father? Why was her mother so sure Des hadn't got him?

'Those women shouldn't have let him go – not without seeing who was getting him.' Jenny couldn't speak of the Cub leaders by name.

Medi said, 'I told Mrs Smithers I was collecting him. I always collect him. She should have kept him till I came.'

'Yes,' said Jenny, but Medi still felt her mother blaming her – and Medi blamed herself.

They went over and over it. Jenny cleaned the sitting room after the kitchen, brushing the carpet with a handbrush. She wouldn't use the vacuum in case she didn't hear the phone. She said she couldn't do nothing, and they drank tea, mug after mug of it, till they ran out of tea-bags. And she rang all Davey's friends again, and her friends and relations, anyone whom Davey knew, and might have gone to. If they answered – only a few did, it was the middle of the night after all – she asked them to check beds, sofas – anywhere. Davey might be sleeping over, she said. Children did that a lot these days. And she asked them to check that he was asleep, if they found him, and not unconscious. She explained about his diabetes. If he hadn't eaten enough or if he'd taken too much insulin, his blood sugar level might have dropped, and he could have fainted – it was called having a hypo. If so they must get a doctor immediately. If they found him feeling faint they should give him a sweet snack.

Davey had taken his kit with him. That was one good thing. Medi and her mum had checked and it wasn't in his bedroom, where he kept it when he was at home. They didn't know how many doses were left in his insulin pen though.

But it was still desperately worrying. Any other child could survive a day or two without food or water, but not diabetics. They had to eat at regular intervals.

Medi still wondered why Jenny didn't ring Des. Why not? She didn't dare ask now. It made her so angry.

They heard St Oswald's clock strike three.

Soon after that Medi must have drifted into sleep because she had a strange dream that she was a swan searching for her brother. She was flying round and round a mountainous terrain, searching for him, but clouds kept getting in the way. She flew through the clouds and round and round the mountain peaks again, but she still couldn't find him. Then she saw a small door in the side of one of the mountains, and she flew down to it. But it was closed and there wasn't a key. Time after time she flew at the door, flapping at it with her huge white wings, till she collapsed beneath it. Then she woke up with eggs underneath her. Two of the eggs had words on them. On one was written *idemedi* in sloping letters. On the other it said *yevadavey*.

Then she really woke up hearing Davey's name – on early morning television. A newsreader was saying that Davey was a quiet, shy boy unlikely to go off with strangers willingly and that police were worried. He mentioned other missing children. A two-year-old boy had disappeared from a shopping precinct in Liverpool. He'd been filmed on the security video though. But nobody had videoed Davey leaving the Beechwood Lane Community Centre. The police were still trying to find out who was the last person to have seen him.

They showed a photograph of Davey, wearing his Cub uniform, the first day he got it.

'I can't believe this is happening to us,' Jenny said, coming into the room with a mug of coffee, and Medi thought she was going to cry, but she gulped and sort of stiffened and concentrated hard on the television screen, where a police spokesman was urging people to keep a lookout and to come forward if they had seen Davey. They showed the Beechwood Lane Community Centre where he had last been seen, and said police had started interviewing the Cubs and the people who had met them last night.

It was on the news again later.

Sarah rang soon after it. She said she was going to join the search party and asked Medi if she was coming.

Medi said, 'What search party?'

Sarah said that Harvey and Gray Parker had organised a group from school. They were going to help the police comb the area, starting with the route Davey might have taken if he'd started walking home by himself.

'He wouldn't have. He would have waited for me.'

'He didn't, Medi. People do sometimes act out of character you know.'

Medi knew she ought to sound grateful. Sarah was unusually quiet on the other end of the phone. Then she said, 'You're not coming then?' and Medi said, 'I don't know. I'll ask my mum.'

She wanted to say, 'What's the point? He's with his dad.' She still thought he was. He must be with Des.

And she didn't like the sound of search parties combing the area. What did they expect to find?

Jenny told Medi to do what she wanted.

Medi told Sarah her mum wanted her to stay at home.

Sarah said, 'Well, if you change your mind, we're starting at the Community Centre and working towards your house.' She added, 'Don't worry, Med, we'll find him . . .' And Medi could feel her thinking . . . dead or alive, relishing the drama of the situation, and she felt a rush of loathing which must have showed on her face because Jenny asked what Sarah had said.

'Nothing really. She just seems so sure something awful has happened.'

'Something awful has happened.'

'Yes but . . .'

She tried again. 'Mum, if Des . . . '

'Medi. Des *hasn't got* Davey. Isn't that clear?'

Then the post arrived.

Her mother ran to pick it up, handed Medi a letter and took her own upstairs.

Medi's was the leaflet the archaeologist had promised her, ages ago it seemed – 'Secrets of the Past' it was called. The archaeologist wished her luck with her project. On the front of the leaflet was a photograph of the skeletons of the two children, their arms round one another, one head resting on the other's shoulder. She stuffed it in her pocket, couldn't bear to read it.

'Mum . . .' She wanted to ask her mother where she thought Davey might have gone, but Jenny was still upstairs reading her post, as she always did. *As she always did.*

It was quiet upstairs but after a while Medi thought she heard her mother's bedroom door opening. Then she heard the bolt on the bathroom door being clicked. So she went upstairs and slipped into her mother's room. There was a gas bill lying on the pink bedcover, that was all, and there was nothing under the pillow, nothing on the dressing table. But she found what she was looking for in the cupboard above the wardrobe, letters. There was a bundle of them from Frank – why hadn't her mother told her Frank wrote to her? There were about three from Des. Reading just one she understood.

She understood her mother's certainty that Davey wasn't with Des.

She understood the secrecy, the mystery, and the deception.

Des couldn't have met Davey from Cubs on Wednesday night.

He couldn't have met Davey because he was in Caldingley Prison.

Prison! A shudder went through her as she read the letter, though the contents were humdrum enough. He'd watched an episode of 'EastEnders'. He'd had a sore throat, seen a robin from a window.

And he sent his love. To her mum. To Medi. To Davey and Joe-boy. He missed them all.

What had he done? There was no mention of that.

He didn't do it. It was wrongful arrest. Like in 'The Railway Children'!

She couldn't bear the thought that the boys' father was a criminal. They would hate that.

She didn't hear water running in the bathroom next door, nor the bolt being drawn back, nor her mother's footsteps on the landing.

'What are you doing?' She was standing in the doorway her eyes on the letter in Medi's hand. It was a stupid question.

'J-just tell me what he's supposed to have done.'

'He took things which weren't his.'

'What do you mean?'

Jenny sat down beside her on the edge of the bed, opened her mouth then closed it again. 'He stole money from the firm he was working for.'

'Why didn't you tell me?'

'I thought it would upset you. It has.' She put her arm round Medi and glanced at the door. 'The boys mustn't know about this.'

The boys. For a few seconds Davey, the missing Davey, had slipped from her mind. Now he was filling it again. So where was he?

'If Des hasn't got Davey, who has?'

Jenny shook her head. She was biting her bottom lip and her eyes were brimming.

Chapter 7

Medi saw the search party when she went to KwikMart to buy tea-bags. Her head felt like the inside of a tumble drier. Now anything seemed possible. Anything. The searchers had reached the field by Oldbridge Road, the one next to Mrs Vogel's, but they were well past her house. They must have searched her garden already. Had the police been to see her? Jenny had told them she thought she was weird and that she'd detained Medi and Joe-boy. At the time Medi had been embarrassed. Now? Well.

It was misty on the far side of the field near the river, but she could see the black and white chequered bands of police officers' caps as they searched the under-growth. There were a lot of policemen, some with tracker dogs, and Medi thought she recognised Sarah's ginger spikes, between Harvey's curls and Gray Parker's baseball cap. They were in the middle of a long line of people moving across the field, poking the ground with sticks. Lots of local people had turned out. The line stretched across the field from the river bank to the road. Two elderly men in flat caps were poking in the hedge that bordered the pavement. One of them said the rain wouldn't help. The other said he thought the police would drag the river next. Medi hurried past. She didn't want to hear any more. It did look like rain, and she hadn't got a mac. She was wearing the cotton top with fringed edges, the one that made her look like a crow, that she'd worn the day she saw the people on the other side of the glass. She knew they'd come to warn her – but she'd misunderstood. She'd expected something to happen to the boys together, not to one of them on his own.

Now the sky was darkening and the mist near the river seemed to be rolling this way. It was hard not to despair. In her pocket was the leaflet that had arrived that morning, on its cover a picture of the child skeletons – *'Aged between six and ten buried in a last embrace, telling of some family tragedy more than 4,000 years ago.'* Like the babes in the wood. A family tragedy. Everything pointed to it.

It started to rain as she came to Mrs Vogel's cottage and stumbled down the steep path. Wychwood. Witchwood. She pounded the biscuit-coloured door and rattled the tarnished brass knocker.

When no one answered she peered through the front window and stepped back in horror! Someone was looking at her! White candles framed a face which seemed to float on a bed of greenery.

It was several seconds before she realised it was her own reflection – in the mirror over the mantelpiece which was covered with evergreens. In fact the room was full of vegetation. There were pot plants all over the place, and dried flowers in jars and boxes. A sheaf of corn stood in one corner of the room and a pot of red-berried branches in the hearth. But the focus of the room was a large round table strewn with branches of yew, and in the middle of the table were twelve white candles in a circle. Of course! The Circle of Light! This must be where they met!

Now fear filled her. Of course. How could she have been so stupid? Of course her mum was right. The place was evil. She could smell it, seeping out of the house through gaps in the ill-fitting window frames. It was a disgusting smell. The house reeked with it. Why hadn't she noticed it yesterday? No wonder Mrs Vogel had kept them outside.

Now Medi rushed round the back, forcing open the side gate. The smell grew stronger, made her eyes sting. Why, why hadn't she noticed it yesterday?

The back door was open. She rushed in.

'What have you done with Davey?'

'Medi!' Mrs Vogel stood open-mouthed – with a plastic jug in one hand and a piece of pink sponge rubber in the other.

And the woman on the chair in front of her sat open-mouthed, foam dripping down her face, spiky curlers in her hair.

Minutes later, feeling stupid and ashamed, Medi made her way to KwikMart. She'd declined Mrs Vogel's offer of tea, stayed only long enough to learn that the police had already called on her and that she didn't mind at all. She wanted to help as much as she could. She said the police had to explore every possible lead. They had to eliminate suspicious people from their enquiries. She could see why Medi's mum suspected her, but she'd have been with the search party herself if she hadn't promised to perm Mrs Merridew's hair.

That was what the smell had been – perming lotion.

Mrs Merridew had been very nice too – nice but dotty. She was having her hair done for Lughnasa, she said. Lughnasa was a sort of harvest festival, one of the old Celtic festivals. The Circle of Light celebrated the old festivals. They liked to thank the Earth Mother for her bounty and Mrs Merridew liked to look her best for them. She showed Medi the corn dollies the ladies of the circle had made. There were a pile of them on the table, little figures made of straw – corn-men and corn-maidens. They had to keep Gulliver away from them, she said. The seagull sat on an upturned broom by the back door. A crow sat on the washing line.

Cars swooshed along the wet road. Head down, hands sunk in her pockets, Medi felt the leaflet she'd received that morning, and half expected skeletons to rise from the paving stones. Or to see a girl and her brothers four thousand years old. She remembered the first time she'd seen them – with Davey by her side. And she remembered the night he'd shouted out in his sleep, 'Don't let them take me away, Medi!'

A crazy thought entered her head. So crazy that she dismissed it.

The KwikMart car park was half empty, except for the crows and rooks who were there in force. As she approached they walked towards her, little men in long

57

black gowns and black caps. They accompanied her to the entrance. She stepped inside and they watched her.

The murder of crows watched her – and she heard the drums.

Chapter 8

Trying to overcome the dread spreading through her, she stepped forward and felt the drums throbbing beneath her feet. *Directly beneath the present superstore lay a sacred enclosure or henge. The circle had one narrow entrance.* Filled with foreboding, she stepped back.

Where? Where was it? In front of her where the doors were turning with mesmerising slowness? Was that why Davey was afraid of them? Had he sensed something that other people were unaware of? Now she could feel their power – had only to step forward to find out.

Where *was* Davey?

Did the doors mark the entrance to the circle?

Were the superstore doors on the site of the ancient entrance?

Had Davey somehow activated them? She pushed the thought aside.

Caw! Caw! More crows dropped from the sky and joined the crowd in front of the doorway. She shuddered as one of them brushed against her legs.

'Go away!' A few rose into the air and hung there like rags, but they dropped again. And more descended from a sky black with crows. And more flew in to take their places, darkening the sky, filling the air with their rackety cries. Then they descended and joined the black throng at her feet.

Cark! Cark! Cwark! Cwark!

'Go away!' They took no notice.

Cark! Cark! They were urging her forward, sweeping her forward with their stiff wings – and part of her wanted to go forward, wanted to step inside those doors. Wanted to see those ghostly figures again.

Round and round went the doors – and she heard the drums, a bass rhythm to the birds' rising chorus. Scrawk! Scrawk!

And on the other side of the doors, checkout girls worked like robots at the tills, and shoppers hurried to and fro, their only worry apparently whether they could steer their bulky trolleys without crashing into each other. Red-coated supervisors checked prices and a baby cried.

A pointed beak nudged her legs – and she knew she had to get out! Had to!

'*Go away!*' She turned and the birds rose in a black cloud.

All except one.

It stood in front of her now, opening and closing its horny beak.

Cark! She saw its grey tongue wagging.

Saw it walking towards her, urging her backwards, towards the doors.

'I can't do it!'

Cawn't! It mocked her.

Coward! Its round eyes stared into hers. Held hers.

Forcing herself to look at the ground she saw its scaly toes.

Then she stepped to the right.

It jumped to the right.

She stepped left.

It jumped left.

So she stood there refusing to move till, after what seemed an age, it flew onto the roof of the building.

It didn't follow her home, thank goodness, but as she passed the cemetery a magpie flew out of a fir tree. One for sorrow.

'What happened to you? You look like a scarecrow!' Jenny was appalled by Medi's appearance.

WPC Donkin didn't comment, but she looked at Medi searchingly. Medi didn't recognise her at first. She was at the sink rinsing cups and she wasn't wearing a jacket or a police hat. She had curly red hair. She said she was about to give Jenny a briefing and that she'd like Medi to listen. She was pleased to say they had a lot more information now. They'd interviewed lots of people already and built up a picture of Davey's movements from the moment he'd arrived at Cubs. He must have left earlier than they had previously thought. Mrs Bentley now remembered looking at her watch when Davey was fussing about a leaf. She'd even thought about taking him home to get it, he'd been so keen to get points for his six. Had Medi any idea what he was on about?

The holly leaf. The skeleton leaf! Medi rushed upstairs.

It was in the pocket of the jacket she'd been wearing

yesterday. Intact. Perfect. Examining it, she caught sight of her reflection in the dressing-table mirror. No wonder her mother had stared. She did look like a scarecrow.

'But it scared me.'

'Who are you talking to, Medi?' Joe-boy wandered in from his bedroom, sucking Bagga. He'd just woken up. It was still quite early.

'Who scared you, Medi?'

'Nobody.'

Joe-boy followed her downstairs and said, 'Medi forgot to give Davey his leaf, Mummy, but she didn't mean to. She just forgot.'

Jenny said Medi had forgotten to get tea-bags too.

WPC Donkin said the police now thought that Davey had left the building on his own, to go after Medi and get his leaf. He must have been fibbing about his daddy collecting him. It was perhaps a bit of wishful thinking, quite understandable in the circumstances. Apparently he'd been seen on the Oldbridge Road by several people at round about seven o'clock. Some people thought they'd seen him in the KwikMart car park, and most importantly, the police thought they might have video of him just outside the entrance to the store.

WPC Donkin wanted Medi and her mum and Joe-boy to look at some security video. It seemed that there were cameras covering both the car park and inside the store. They were there to deter thieves and the police had brought the video – and a video recorder – with them. Another policeman was setting it up in the sitting room. It would be ready in a minute. While they were waiting the police woman said there was one other lead. There had been reports of a strange man in the area, though nobody recalled seeing Davey with him. He was tall and fair with a moustache. Did he remind them of anyone? Jenny said Des, the boys' father was fair, but she'd already explained about him. WPC Donkin nodded. She said the police had asked men to come forward to be identified and eliminated from their enquiries and there had been a lot of response. They hoped the stranger would come forward soon. The public were being very helpful.

WPC Donkin was upbeat. Medi felt worse, a complete failure. She put her hands in her pockets and pricked her finger.

The film wasn't clear. It was grey rather than black and white and it jerked a lot, but Medi and Jenny were almost certain that the little boy in the Cub uniform standing in the car park, just in front of the revolving doors, was Davey.

Joe-boy said, 'Davey didn't like the doors. He didn't like the time-machine.'

WPC Donkin said, 'What does he mean?'

Medi explained – about Davey's fear of the doors and their pretend game.

Joe-boy said, 'We time-travelled to see the dinosaurs.'

Medi didn't say anything else, but she studied the video intently. She saw the crows. Had they mobbed Davey, scared him as they'd scared her, made him fall against the doors perhaps? It was difficult to see whether he had stepped into the doors or not. The film became very blurred at that point as if someone had fast-forwarded it, though they hadn't. What *had* happened? The policeman said the evening sun, low in the western sky at that time, had whited out part of the film. It was very annoying, just the bit they needed to watch.

There was no sign of Davey in the store. Medi watched nearly an hour of film, saw herself and Joe-boy. Davey must have been outside the store while they were inside choosing sweets. If only they'd looked out of the windows. If only . . .

They looked at the video tape again from the beginning.

'Look at the birds, Medi.' Joe-boy pointed at the screen, where the crows did seem to be hustling Davey forward, and this time he did seem to be stepping inside the revolving doors, not standing still.

They re-wound the tape and looked again.

Yes, he was stepping into the doorway.

'But he didn't come out the other side.' Medi didn't realise she'd spoken aloud, till one of the policemen, he was called PC Lawless, said, 'Well we can't say for sure because of the white-out and the cameras inside don't record everything. There are blind spots.'

There wasn't a camera actually focused where people came in, it seemed. The outside camera filmed people stepping from the car park into the door. The focus of the nearest indoor camera didn't quite reach the door. So there was film of Davey stepping into the revolving doors, but none of him actually walking round in them, and none of him stepping out.

'That's what I said,' said Medi.

There was no sign of him inside the store. It was very strange. The crazy thought she'd had earlier seemed less crazy, but she still couldn't share it with anyone. Her mother already thought she was useless. If she knew what she was thinking, she'd have her certified. Perhaps Jenny was right. But she had to go back to the store. She had to put her idea to the test.

She said she was going back for the tea-bags.

Chapter 9

But PC Lawless followed her out of the room, saying he would take her to KwikMart in the car. Medi said no thank you, she preferred to walk, but he said, 'Look at the weather, love.'

He opened the front door to a waterfall. Rain was cascading off the front porch and bouncing off the path below. He handed her his raincoat. Then he dashed out saying he'd open the door for her. As she followed, there was a rumble of thunder.

The sky was bruise grey and as they drove out of Poppy Gardens it got so dark that PC Lawless switched on the headlights. Glancing at his face, Medi could see that he wasn't a lot older than she was, though he'd grown a moustache to make himself look older, and he talked non-stop, trying to be grown-up and reassuring. She wished he would shut up. He said she might find the store confusing because it was being searched thoroughly. Every corner was being looked into, every cardboard box, every plastic container – just in case Davey had gone in there. He might have fallen asleep while hiding perhaps, or even become ill. Medi's mother had told the police about Davey being diabetic.

The windscreen wipers beat furiously. As they passed Futurama Computers there was a flash of lightning. Medi wished the man would stick to driving, but he carried on talking. He said they'd know more later when experts had examined the video. They'd probably make a copy of it, an improved copy, so that they could see more clearly what went on. Then they'd analyse it. It was amazing what they could do these days.

When they reached the car park he drove right up to the covered causeway, and said he would park the car as near as he could then come and find her. She got out and he drove off.

There weren't many shoppers, but the crows were waiting for her. They lined the causeway – under cover – they weren't daft. More stood round the doors, croaking importantly, with shoulders hunched. Here she is. Here she is. Knew she'd be back. Told you so.

The rain was like glass on either side of her. She felt as if she were in a tunnel from which there was no escape. But now she didn't want to escape. Her mind was made up. She had to try this. So she strode forward stepping on lines, stepping on squares, stepping on litter, stepping on the brass plaque commemorating the prehistoric site, stepping on anything. She didn't care. Intent only on going forward, she put one foot in front of the other, seeing only the doors in front of her.

And one crow, silent now, walked beside her.

The throng round the doors divided to let her through. Then she stood for a few moments, watching the activity beyond the doors, the thorough search taking place – people taking tins off shelves, people standing on steps to look in high places and crouching to search the spaces under the tills. One man manoeuvred a snake of trolleys into a space near the windows. Others dismantled it, looking carefully in each basket. And there were tracker dogs sniffing, searching for Davey.

He isn't there. You won't find him. I lost him. I must find him.

Now was the time. She saw the warning. DO NOT PUSH EXCEPT IN AN EMERGENCY. *This is an emergency*. She thrust the palms of her hands against the glass and pushed hard – and the doors stopped.

She pushed harder.

Nothing happened.

People were staring at her now. Some were pointing. In the corner of her eye she saw a supervisor approaching. In the car park she saw Mrs Vogel and Mrs Merridew with a towel round her head. *Widdershins*. The word came into her head. *They're going the wrong way, that's the trouble*. That's what she'd said. *Widdershins*. They should be going the other way like the sun and the moon.

So Medi turned round – just as the supervisor reached the doors – and gathering all her strength, she thrust the palms of her hands against the glass. There was a second of resistance then the doors were moving, gathering speed, spinning! And she was spinning, conscious only of the sound of rushing wind.

Half an hour later, a distraught Jenny, a stunned PC Lawless, WPC Donkin and several members of the CID, were all watching more store video, this time of Medi filmed by the car park camera as she stepped into the revolving doors.

They saw her pushing anti-clockwise. They saw her turning round and pushing again, in the opposite direction. They saw a crow fly into the doors. Then they saw a flash and a blur of crackling lines. Then nothing at all. The rest of the tape was blank.

They re-wound it and played it again. They couldn't explain it, couldn't blame the sun this time. It wasn't a white-out. PC Lawless said, 'One second she was there, then she wasn't.' He said that several times.

On the second re-play Joe-boy, coming in from the kitchen, said, 'Medi said it was a time-machine. She said it was.' He sucked Bagga and Jenny stroked his hair.

She said she wasn't letting Joe-boy out of her sight, ever. First her son, then her husband and now her daughter – they had all disappeared. Who could she trust? She thought Medi would have been safe with a policeman, and her husband with prison officers, but he'd given them the slip on the way to the new prison they were taking him to.

Joe-boy said, 'Who's in prison?'

Jenny said, 'No one.'

PC Lawless buried his head in his hands, and WPC Donkin murmured to him that there had been a phone call, just after he'd left for KwikMart – to say that Des had given his guards the slip on the way to a different prison.

* * *

And Medi, crouching in tall grass, looked all around her at a monochrome landscape, a patchwork in tones of sepia, like an old photograph. But she wasn't looking at an old photograph – she knew that – she was in the past. She was at the foot of the ancient mound.

Chapter 10

There was a fence right round it. That was something she hadn't expected. The totems of the outer circle were fence posts and attached to them were panels of woven sticks, which formed a gated enclosure. She was clutching one of the gateposts; she could feel its carved surface beneath her fingers. And through the opening she could see the mound rising steeply in front of her, and another ring of totems about halfway up, and a single totem on the summit crowned with a deer's antlers. The totems cast long shadows across the mound, for in the east the sun was a copper dome.

There was no sound at all. The quietness was uncanny, a presence flowing round her, enfolding her. Listening, she shivered – with the cold but also the wonder of it all – and she glanced at her watch. Twelve noon, but it wasn't twelve noon. She held it to her ear. It had stopped. It was as if everything had stopped.

Then she jumped, as she remembered why she had come. *Davey!* For several minutes she had forgotten him completely. The past – or was it the future? – had slipped away like a dream in the morning. Davey was in her head now, but sliding already, she had to concentrate hard to keep him there – *Davey, Davey. I must find you.* She stood up and now the surrounding landscape engrossed her, as it took shape before her – rapidly, like one of those magic painting books where you simply apply water and wait! But it was the rising sun sharpening the edges of things and filling shapes with colour. It was the domed sun, streaking the eastern sky with copper and gold. It was the sun greening the fields and blackening the forest edge, patching the landscape with brown and blue and red. Red – moving towards her! A herd of deer!

Cwark! A crow landed on the post above her. Just beneath it the yellow eyes of a wolf's head blazed.

Cwark! The crow took off – soared high over a stripy stubble field. Then it came down on something green, a roof! One of several roofs. There was a circle of buildings in a hollow beneath her. A settlement! Was that where Davey was? *Davey!* Taking a biro from her pocket she wrote his name on her hand. Then she started to count the buildings, got to twenty, as the mist which must have covered them before rolled aside to reveal a river. She could see that now – a serpent coiling round the settlement – gleaming as the sun caught its back. Was Davey in one of those buildings? Were there people there or animals or both? She was sure she could hear the snuffle of sleeping pigs and smoke curled from the chimney of a building whose doorway faced outwards faced her in fact. She was looking straight at it.

And someone or something was looking at her! She saw something move.

Moving back instantly, so that she was again behind the fence peering through, she saw a couple of dogs sniffing around – so that was what she'd seen. But were they dogs? One of them threw back its head and howled. She kept as still as she could, but the sound had alerted other animals. A cow bellowed and the pigs grunted, and as she listened, wondering how she could get into the settlement without being seen or heard or smelt, the air was suddenly filled with bird cries – trilling, trebling, honking, quacking, and mostly the rackety clamour of rooks and crows from the woodlands.

The dawn chorus – so it was now or never, before the inhabitants woke up – but even as she stepped forward she saw that it was too late.

Clearly now, someone was standing in the doorway of the building opposite.

A girl was looking towards the mound, was looking in fact straight at Medi.

Their eyes met, the girl dropped to her knees and thumped the earth with her hands.

Still as a stone, she had been watching for some time and had seen Medi suddenly appear on the mound – on the belly of Earth Mother – and to the girl that could only mean one thing. Dark and stockily built, like all the Corn People, she had seen folk with fair hair and fair skin and with dark hair and dark skin. She had seen folk with red hair and pale speckled skin, but only once before had she seen black hair and skin as pale as Medi's. Only once before had she seen those strange garments. So this must be Crow Maiden.

For Medi in her fringed black clothes from Oxfam, with the fringes fluttering in the morning breeze, looked bird-like. And her shadow, stretching across the mound looked bird-like. And there were birds all around her though she did not know it. On each sacred totem perched a crow and were not crows messengers from the Dark Place?

The crows cawed and the girl was afraid.

This Crow Maiden was obviously Earth Mother's Messenger. But why had she come? To give or take away?

Fearfully she began to speak. 'Crow Maiden, I beg you.' She thumped the earth with the palms of her hands and amazingly Medi understood.

'Crow Maiden, I beg you to save my brothers in blood.'

And Medi was entranced, certain now that the girl was the one she had seen in the car park, the one she wanted to meet, the one *she* wanted to ask for help. And now alerted by the girl's voice, other figures appeared, ducking their heads as they emerged from low doorways, some clutching the edges of animal skins wrapped round their shoulders, some wearing tunics – and men she thought, in breeches. Rubbing their eyes as they came into the sunlight, they looked first at the girl, and then at the mound and Medi.

But they weren't seeing her – at least Medi thought they weren't – because their eyes weren't focused so directly on her as the girl's eyes.

'O Visitor from the Dark Place, help us. Visitor from the Dark Place, save my brothers in blood.'

The girl beat the earth with a desperate rhythm. And

the others copied her, making the earth tremble.

'O Visitor from the Dark Place, help us . . .'

Medi counted nearly a hundred people on their knees, praying *to her*.

'Save our brothers in blood.'

And she didn't know what to do.

Then she saw a man emerging from the same building that the girl had come out of. There was a murmur which may have been, 'The chief, the chief,' but then everyone fell silent. There was something about him that commanded respect, though he looked downcast and was dressed no differently from the other men.

The girl spoke to him, pointing to the mound. What was she saying? He followed her pointed finger. Did he see what the girl saw? Medi wasn't sure, she thought perhaps not, but he did drop to his knees and thump the ground as she had done.

Then he got up and walked swiftly to a building on the other side of the settlement. Everyone remained silent and still, till he reappeared – with an amazing figure, over two metres high, who walked stiffly beside him, in a long golden dress.

'Corn Priest! Corn Priest!' The word went round. 'The chief's fetched Corn Priest.'

Much of his height was an enormous head-dress that swayed as he walked. It made his head look like a blazing sun, and a staff in his right hand bore the same sun emblem. When the two men reached the girl, she spoke to the priest who listened solemnly then murmured to a group of men beside him. Then they hurried off, in the direction the priest had come from and he turned towards the mound and raised his arms.

'Earth Mother,

Who creates all things.

We thank you and you shall see our thanks!'

His words boomed and echoed as if from deep inside him. He said it again and again, till the men he'd sent off reappeared, with what Medi could only describe as an enormous corn dolly. It was like the little figures she had seen in Mrs Vogel's kitchen, but much much bigger, the size of a man in fact or more likely a woman. It certainly needed the four men to carry it, which they did high above their heads, till they stood before the priest. Then led by him, they started to climb the mound, and after a few minutes they were standing in front of her!

Now she could see that everything the priest wore was made of woven straw. The chief and his daughter stood on either side of him. Surely they could all see her as clearly as she could see them? But the priest seemed to look *through* her as he raised his voice once more.

'Earth Mother, Behold our sacrifice!

Earth Mother,

At sundown,

Corn Maiden will return to you!'

Corn Maiden? The corn dolly presumably?

Medi still didn't know what to do. So she just stood there, perfectly still, feeling the girl's eyes on her. Though only she could see her, they all seemed to be involving her in some sort of bargain. They would make a gift of the Corn Maiden and she would – what?

'Save my sons in blood!' The anguished cry came from the man, the chief, the girl's father. He was on his knees now, and so was the girl. 'Save my brothers in blood!'

And as they both thumped the ground in supplication, the truth dawned. The girl's brothers, the man's sons – so they were father and daughter – were ill. And they thought she could save them.

'Save my sons in blood!' The man beat the ground with his hands and so did the girl beside him. So did the crowd behind them led by the Corn Priest. Their cries and their beating grew to a frenzy, making them unaware of an even odder figure approaching.

A gigantic crow was striding towards them from the direction of the river.

'The shaman.' Someone had seen it. The word went round. 'Crowman has come from across the water.'

'To save our brothers in blood,' someone said. 'To save the tribe.'

'Silence! Heed him not!' All eyes now turned towards the Corn Priest, who stood in the crow's path. 'Come no further, Old One!'

But the gigantic crow continued to approach.

'Come no further, Old Fellow! Your ways are not our ways!'

Still the crow came forward.

The Corn Priest held up his golden staff but the crow figure swept past. Now all eyes were on the amazing figure they called Crowman. He stood not far from Medi now. She could see the toes of his human feet. He seemed not to see her, but it was hard to tell. A mask of shiny feathers covered the top half of his face. A horny beak vibrated as he spoke.

'The gods are angry!' His voice was surprisingly high-pitched.

'The gods are angry with your false gifts.' He lifted a winged arm and pointed at the Corn Maiden still borne high by her carriers.

'Corn Maiden!' His squeaky voice trembled with scorn. 'Straw Maiden! The gods want flesh and blood!'

Chapter 11

A man dressed as a crow! A muppet! He ought to have been funny, but no one found him funny, least of all Medi.

'The gods demand blood not straw!' he squeaked, and people cowered.

'Earth Mother will have the blood of a ram!' boomed the Corn Priest.

'The gods want human blood!' piped the Crowman.

There was silence then, as people looked from one to the other. Then the Corn Priest stepped forward so that he towered over the crow figure. 'Your ways are old ways, old man! Your old gods failed us!'

He turned to the people. 'You have heard how they failed us. You have heard of the long dark moons of ice and snow when the hunters came back empty-handed. When half the tribe starved. Year after year after year they starved – despite human sacrifice.' Now people shuffled uneasily.

'You know that the tribe was dying,' the priest pressed home his vantage, 'till we became farmers, till we became settlers, till we became the Corn People!' He raised his staff. 'Till we learned to grow our food, how to rear our food, so we always had food – even during the long dark moons of the frost and snow. And,' he turned towards the mound, 'we turned to kinder gods.'

There was a murmur of assent.

'Earth Mother is kind!' the Corn Priest asserted. 'Earth Mother has shown us new ways. New kinder ways to sacrifice.' He gestured towards the Corn Maiden, still held high by the four bearers.

'We give corn to Earth Mother, and Earth Mother gives to us. We shall sacrifice the Corn Maiden, today at our Gathering Feast.' He looked defiantly at the Crowman who had turned his back and was looking hard at the house where the boys lay ill.

'So why have your sons in blood got the sickness?' he whined, turning towards the boys' father. 'The gods are angry, that is why. Earth Mother does not want the Corn Maiden. She wants a maid.'

His weird voice once again held the crowd.

'Life for life. Flesh for flesh. Return to the old ways. Give thanks to Earth Mother with blood – or the sickness might spread.'

A man said, 'Whose blood? Which maid? Tell us Crowman.'

He didn't answer, but Medi could feel his eyes on her and knew he was seeing her! Then she was distracted for a moment – by a loud caw – as a crow landed on the post above her. Buffeted by the wind, it swayed from side to side, clinging on with its long toes – and a breast-feather came loose. The feather whirled in the air above her for a moment, then it flew away, dipping and lifting, floating on the wind.

And she saw the Crowman watching it, saw everyone watching it. All eyes were on that crow feather, which fluttered and twirled, then landed at the feet of the chief's daughter.

'Crow Maiden has chosen,' squeaked the Crowman.

The crowd gasped. 'Keira! She has chosen Keira!'

The girl stared at the feather now touching her feet.

'Keira!' Murmurs passed from one to another. The chief's daughter. The feather was a sign. Medi didn't understand. A sign of what? How could a random feather be a sign of anything?

The Crowman said no more. He didn't need to it seemed. The sign was so obvious. The girl was still looking down at the feather. Her father had covered his face with his hands. Then the Crowman picked up the feather and with his winged arm he began to draw a circle on the ground round the girl. One young man rushed forward with a cry of 'No! No!' but other men pulled him back.

The priest stepped forward. He was pulled back.

The Crowman completed the circle.

Then Medi, watching, could hardly believe what she saw. The Corn Maiden's bearers gradually lowered her to the ground. Why were they listening to this madman? The Corn Priest, looking round for help to raise her again, found no one to meet his eyes. Everyone was disappearing now, into their huts. He began to drag the Corn Maiden away, and realisation dawned. Medi understood what everyone else had understood instantly. The girl, Keira, had been chosen as a sacrifice – and the Crowman said she, Medi, the Crow Maiden, had chosen her.

Keira was still on her knees. She didn't move. It was

as if there was a fence round her, not an invisible circle. Medi felt sick. When would this terrible thing happen?

It mustn't happen. Someone must stop it. But now the Crowman was speaking to the girl who got up. Then she went into the hut with her father, and the Crowman strode away towards the woods.

As women appeared with food, and people started to gather in front of their huts, Medi realised she was hungry. It must be breakfast time. As they ate, people glanced at the chief's hut – but no one came out of it. No one talked much. A heavy silence hung over the settlement. Medi imagined the scene inside the hut – and wondered what was the matter with the two sick boys. She imagined their mother beside them – she obviously hadn't left their side – the father and the girl, all of them too sad and worried to think of food, and she was filled with a sense of hopelessness.

They would die. Medi remembered the photograph of the skeletons, and the words beneath them. *Curled close together, they bear witness to a human tragedy four thousand years ago*. And she remembered reading of another grave of *a young adult* nearby. Now she could guess whose that was. How upset Davey had been just to read about it. *Davey!*

He wasn't on the mound. She searched every inch of it, even walking inside the ditch which surrounded the second circle of totems. It was as deep as she was tall and the grass inside it was long. There was no sign of him. When she reached the top, she surveyed the scene below her and wondered what she'd hoped to find. Davey, of course, but failing that some sort of clue – his yellow Cub scarf or a woggle, a trainer print in the mud. There was no mud. Clearly it hadn't rained for some time. The ground was dry. The harvest had been gathered. Hadn't the Corn Priest said something about a Gathering Feast today? Would she get a chance to search the settlement then when they were all up here perhaps celebrating?

Looking at the wolf's head carved on the totem in front of her, she remembered Davey's voice. *Medi! Look behind you! There's a wolf!* And she feared for Davey as she'd always feared for him, perhaps wandering now where real wolves roamed.

Then turning to scan the surrounding landscape, she saw someone climbing the mound.

Chapter 12

It was the girl, Keira, carrying something. As she got closer she slowed down a bit, seemed nervous in fact, and when she reached the top she knelt down and stared at Medi's feet; she seemed afraid to look straight at her. Then she began to take things out of a shallow basket. There was a beaker and a plate, both decorated with an intricate pattern of lines, and something wrapped in leaves. She stood the beaker on the grass, making it secure by scraping away some earth, then she unfolded the leaves – and arranged the contents on the plate. She put a pile of nuts in the middle, and a circle of just-ripe blackberries round the outside, and some round things which looked like those oatcakes called flapjacks, in the four quarters of the plate. Then she offered it to Medi with outstretched arms.

Medi longed to eat the food – she was starving hungry – but wondered whether she ought to. If it was an offering to the Earth Mother, shouldn't she just look at it, or place it at the base of one of the totems, the one at the summit maybe? The girl might be shocked if Medi suddenly wolfed the food down.

But the girl was nodding as if urging her on, and she was saying something – it sounded like *blaanda* as she pointed to the flapjack things.

So Medi started to eat.

The blaanda weren't bad, a bit smoky on the outside, but they tasted like flapjacks. They'd been sweetened with honey though, not golden syrup. She could taste the honey even more in the drink which was very sweet. The girl poured this into the beaker from a leather bottle which hung from a girdle round her waist. She wore a tunic made of reddish-brown cloth, the same colour as some small sheep grazing in a field nearby. The blackberries tasted sour, so she tried one of the nuts next. The girl had shelled some of them, and she shelled the others now – banging them deftly between two flat stones.

And from time to time she looked up at Medi with shy anxious glances. Mostly though, she stared at Medi's feet – seemed fascinated by her trainers! The girl's feet were brown and bare.

As Medi ate she thought about Davey, and wondered if the girl could help her find him. Perhaps she'd seen him? Medi smiled and the girl smiled a quick smile back, but most of the time she looked worried and Medi wished she didn't. Then she remembered what was on the girl's mind and wondered why she didn't look more worried.

'Keira?' She was about to say, 'Have you seen a little boy, a stranger . . .?'

But as soon as Medi said her name, the girl started to speak. 'Keira begs the Earth Mother to save her brothers.' She touched the ground with her forehead.

'Keira offers her life, for the lives of her brothers.' She touched the ground again. Then she looked up, and

Medi, seeing her own reflection in the girl's huge dark pupils, wanted to say, 'No, there's no point!' – but she didn't say anything.

Find Davey and get home before it happened – that's all she could do.

So she said, 'Take me to your brothers,' because that would get her into the settlement.

As the girl led the way Medi kept a lookout, especially as they approached the huts. The area round them reminded her of the allotments near the school, except that the main crop seemed to be weeds! There were lots of small plots, some full of nettles, some of dandelion and goose grass – the stuff that stuck to you when you walked by it – and she thought she recognised a leggy grey-green weed called fat hen.

The buildings though, weren't like the shacks on the allotments. All built to the same pattern, they looked neat and sturdy. The low walls were made of woven panels and the bright green roofs which nearly reached the ground, were made of grass that was still growing.

Some people stared at Keira as she passed by, others averted their eyes. As far as Medi could tell no one else saw her, so she was able to look at them closely. Most of them had the same shining black hair as the girl and her stocky build, but a few were taller and thinner with brown hair and rounder faces. A couple of dogs – they were grey and wolf-like – came up and sniffed her, which was a bit alarming, but when the girl spoke to them they loped off. Most people were still standing round their huts. A few were still eating breakfast. Two children were sharing a bowl of something which looked like porridge, dipping into it with wooden spoons.

Some people were working. A leathery-skinned old man sat on his own with his back to a building, chipping away at a flint. There was a bow at his side, and another arrow by it, shaped like a leaf. He seemed to be copying it. Further along a group of men sat round a pile of antlers hacking bits off them, and another man was sprinkling something – it smelt disgusting – over a deerskin stretched on a wooden rack. There were several racks with different skins stretched over them in the gaps between the huts. Beyond them, in the middle of the settlement, were more enclosures, and she glimpsed the movements of animals behind wattle hurdles. She thought she could smell pigs; she was sure she could hear them snuffling and thought she could see some more sheep too.

Then the girl stopped outside a hut – it was the one directly opposite the entrance to the circle – with a porch and an inner doorway covered with a sheepskin. And with a gesture to Medi, she stepped inside, letting the skin drop behind her. So Medi was left staring at the curly wool and listening to the murmuring within. But she couldn't make out anything that was said.

Was Davey inside? She had been keeping a lookout all the time, but had seen no sign of him so far. She examined the porch. There was no sign of him here either – or was there? There was something about the place which reminded her of him.

On the wall leaned a garden tool – or was it a weapon? – a sharp-edged stone anyway, bound to a wooden staff with leather. On a ledge was a dish of soft clay with what looked like marbles in it – about thirty in all, and all different sizes. She was wondering if it was some sort of a calendar, when the girl appeared again, holding back the door cover for Medi to enter.

At first she could hardly see anything, it was so dark. She was aware of a circle of posts holding up the roof and a fire in the centre of the floor but not much else. Then it went even darker as the girl dropped the door covering behind them, and the only light was in the centre of the room, beneath the chimney hole. The fire was low, not much more than a smouldering log really, and its blue-grey smoke thickened the darkness. Then the girl was by her side steering her between the posts and round the fire to the other side of the hut.

'My father, Dal. My mother, Kara. I bring you Earth Mother's Messenger. She is among us now.'

As her eyes adjusted, Medi could see two still figures near the wall. Could they see her? They bowed their heads towards her – but she thought not. They looked as the blind looked, with a wandering gaze. One was the man she had seen earlier; he was standing. The other must be his wife; she was kneeling by the two boys, who lay on a raised bed of hay covered with grey fur.

Medi wouldn't have noticed the boys, if their pale faces hadn't stood out from the darkness. They were motionless and at first she thought they were dead. Then she saw the skins covering them rise and fall. So one of them at least was breathing. She watched for a bit longer, kneeling to see better, and she thought she saw the boy nearest to her take a shallow breath. The fur beneath him was damp as if he'd wet the bed.

His mother wiped his face gently with a pad of moss.

Medi could feel Keira watching her, could feel her wanting her to do something for the boys, but she was still thinking mostly of Davey, she still had the sense that he was near. There was something in the air. She scanned the room again – sniffed. That was it, a smell! *The* smell! The nail varnish smell of Davey when he'd been ill, before they knew what was the matter with him, before he'd got treatment. It was the ultra-sweet *ketonic* smell of sugar saturating the body, leaking out of it.

'Davey!' she called out. He was here, must be! Standing up, she looked all around, frightened now. If he smelt like that he was ill, was hyper, was probably in a coma!

'Davey!' Now, she half-ran round the room, calling his name, looking behind the walls that divided the sleeping area from the cooking area, the cooking area from the storage area – looking everywhere frantically, following her nose. She peered into shadowy corners. She lifted animal skins. She rummaged in the hay that formed their beds – and she sniffed. She sniffed everywhere she looked. She climbed up several rungs of the ladder that led to the roof-space and she sniffed up there. Then she climbed down the ladder and, more slowly now, almost reluctantly, she walked back to the boys – because that's where her nose led her. The smell was stronger there.

It was them. The smell was coming from them. She knelt down to make sure, putting her head close to theirs, and she smelt their sweet sickly breath. There was no mistaking it. Then she felt the damp covers beneath them – they had wet their bed and she knew without a doubt what was the matter with them. She knew why they were going to die.

They were in a diabetic coma – it was obvious – because their bodies couldn't deal with sugar. Like Davey. Davey.

So she hadn't found Davey. Hadn't found Davey. Hadn't found Davey. That was all she could think of.

But the girl was shaking her elbow. 'Keira begs the Earth Mother to save her brothers. Keira offers her life for the life of her brothers.'

Words came into Medi's head – instructions – because she knew them off by heart.

What to do in the case of coma. *Do not force liquids down the patient.* Okay. *Ring for an ambulance.* Oh yes! *Inject with Actrapid insulin. Give intravenous fluid.*

She could feel Keira's eyes on her beseeching her to do something, but there was nothing she could do. She hadn't got insulin. She couldn't give intravenous fluid. The air was heavy with silence and dark with smoke. Then someone behind her lifted the door covering and a shaft of light enabled her to see the boys more clearly. They were dark haired with lovely long eyelashes, but they reminded her of blond Davey and Joe-boy. It was their angelic expressions as they slept. Were they just sleeping? They were horribly still.

In the silence a few outside noises were distinct. A cow bellowed. A pig squealed. The arrowmaker carried on his steady chip-chip. Every now and then someone shouted, and was quickly shushed. Mostly voices were low. What was happening outside? What preparations were taking place for this Gathering Feast? What time was it now?

Suddenly the sun slanted in through the chimney hole, spot-lighting Keira, whose eyes never left her brothers. And Medi wished she could do something to save her at least from death at the hands of the hideous Crowman. What could she do now? When was this horrendous harvest festival supposed to begin?

'Keira . . .' As Medi spoke, so did someone else, and Keira turned to face the doorway.

Chapter 13

The shaman had come for Keira. His hideous crow
figure filled the doorway blocking the light, but she
could tell that he was angry, could see below his beak, a
jaw-nerve twitching.

'Don't go. Stay with your brothers.' Medi appealed to
Keira, still kneeling beside her, but she was rooted to the
spot, transfixed by the Crowman's gaze.

'Come. Leave Crow Maiden to tend your brothers.'
Medi had to remind herself that he meant *her*! That he
was claiming her as a helpmate!

'The gods are just. They may save your brothers.
Now is the time for sacrifice. Life for life. Come.'

Keira stood up – like an automaton. Her parents
seemed paralysed.

Medi stood up. 'Don't go to him, Keira.'

The girl hesitated.

'Don't go, Keira. Earth Mother does not want you to
die.'

The nerve in the shaman's jaw jumped. 'Come,' he
said.

Medi said, 'I bring messages from the Earth Mother.
She does not want her children to die.'

The Crowman's mouth twisted with barely controlled
anger. 'The gods give life for life! Come.' He jerked his
head towards Keira. 'You must prepare yourself.'

'*No!*' The strength of Medi's reply surprised even her as she stepped between Keira and the Crowman. '*No! Earth Mother does not want blood sacrifice! Earth Mother does not want the return of the Old Ways! Earth Mother will receive the Corn Maiden not the Maid.*'

'*Medi!*'

What happened next was confusing. Someone said her name and she turned to see who. There was a roar and a scream, a scuffle. More men appeared, their faces covered. Someone yelled, 'Look out!'

Dal fell to the floor and Medi, looking up, saw Davey in the roof-space!

'Don't let them, Medi!' He yelled even louder this time, but by the time she realised what he meant – and got over her shock and delight at seeing him again – it was too late. The shaman had gone and so had Keira. By the time Davey had scrambled down the ladder and they had both rushed outside, the Crowman and the girl were out of sight.

'Where have they gone?' Medi yelled at the crowd round the door, but no one answered. She looked towards the river. 'Someone must have seen them go! Where? Where are they?'

Davey said, 'They can't see us, Medi. Or hear us. Only certain people can. *We* must do something.' He was distraught and blamed himself for waking up and yelling at just the wrong moment. He wanted to save Keira. He wanted to know what was the matter with the boys.

But Medi's priorities were different. She'd found

Davey. She'd done what she'd come to do. So she said, 'We can't do anything. We must go home now.'

They had to get back to the circle and make the magic work in reverse. But Davey wouldn't move. Dal was coming out of the hut. He was holding his head and looked dazed – and a young man with dark flowing hair was breaking free from two older men who were restraining him. It was the young man who had rushed forward when the shaman had first drawn the circle round Keira.

'Over there!' He pointed to the woods behind the settlement. 'Crowman has taken Keira there, to his secret hide-out! We must rescue her!'

Medi noticed the Corn Priest at the edge of the crowd. He nodded at the young man's words, but the arrowmaker was saying that they must do what Crowman said, or the chief's sons would die and the whole tribe would suffer. Dal looked from one to the other. Davey said, 'What does he mean?'

Medi explained about the boys' diabetes.

People looked bewildered. They were afraid of Crowman, that was the trouble. He'd convinced them that sacrificing Keira was the only way to save the boys. He was wrong. Only insulin could save the boys.

'What?'

Davey was nudging her, his face shining! 'I've got my kit, Medi! With Actrapid insulin!'

'You can't use that. You might . . .' Need it yourself, she was going to say, but Davey shot back into the hut. By the time she caught up with him he was kneeling

beside the boys with his Novopen. Kara, the boys'
mother, knelt by them too, unaware of Davey's
presence.

'How much insulin do you think?' said Davey.

There was no arguing with him. Medi looked at the
boys. They were both smaller than Davey. 'Try 12 units
for a start.'

Davey injected the insulin into the thigh of the boy
nearest to him. He did the same to the other boy. Then
they waited. Even Actrapid insulin took at least half an
hour to work – if it was going to. While they were
waiting Medi looked around the hut for water. They
couldn't give it to the boys while they were
unconscious, but they would need lots to drink if they
came round.

She found some in a pouch made of animal skin. It
was hanging on one of the posts, surrounded by bunches
of herbs. She smelt mint and the orangey tang of
coriander. There was more water in a pot in the cooking
area. She picked up a beaker – it looked like the one
Keira had brought to the mound with the honey-
flavoured drink in it – filled it with water, and put it
beside the bed.

'Thanks be to Earth Mother!' Kara's words took her
by surprise. She was watching her sons intently – and
the one nearest her was opening his eyes.

'Dev!' Kara's eyes were brimming with happiness.

'Ari!' The other boy was waking too. 'I give thanks to
Earth Mother.' Kara touched the earth floor with her
forehead. Then she turned back to her sons and kissed

them. Clearly she felt that a miracle had taken place.

When she saw the boys drinking from a beaker – which seemed to hover in mid air! – she again touched the earth and thanked the Earth Mother. Then she ran to the doorway to tell her husband. 'Earth Mother has saved us! Earth Mother has saved our sons!'

The boys, Ari and Dev, were delighted to see Davey. Davey was beside himself with joy

Dal came rushing in. After a few minutes, Medi and Davey followed him, as he carried the boys outside. The crowd gasped and rippled with pleasure.

Medi whispered in Ari's ear. Solemnly he repeated her words.

'Earth Mother wants your thanks, but she does not want blood sacrifice. Earth Mother wants to receive the Corn Maiden in the Dark Place. Earth Mother wants the Corn Priest to lead the Gathering Feast!'

As the crowd listened the Corn Priest moved forward. Then he turned to the people.

'The Corn People thank the Earth Mother. The Corn People will honour the Earth Mother in the New Way! Go fetch the Corn Maiden! Hoist her high!'

Dal took Ari and Dev back into the hut.

The young man, the one who had wanted to rescue Keira earlier, followed him. They had a few words before Dal went inside. When he came out, the two of them and two others set off at a run for the woods.

Davey wanted to go with the search party. Medi forbade him, actually held him firmly by the arm. She said, 'Keira will be all right.'

He said, 'How do you know?'

She didn't know but she was desperate to get him home, which meant getting back to the mound. She said, 'The people are going to celebrate in the new way. They won't let the Crowman do anything to Keira.' It was a chance they had to take. She couldn't take chances with Davey's life. She had to get him home – or he'd be ill. She said so. He'd already had some of his insulin, and he'd given his emergency reserve of Actrapid to Ari and Dev. He wanted to go inside and see them again.

She said, 'Just to say goodbye then.'

But it was as if he hadn't heard her. He said he wanted to make sure the boys were okay.

They were sitting on the hearth stones, eating blaanda, watched by their mother. Davey told them that they should have some milk too and they asked for some. They could see Davey and Medi, but the mother couldn't. Medi followed her when she went to get the milk – to an enclosure behind the hut where a girl was milking a sheep into a wooden bucket. The girl was dark and muscular like Keira. The bucket looked as if it had been hollowed out of a tree trunk. It was about half full of milk and when the spurt of milk from the sheep's udder slowed to a trickle, the girl greeted Kara with a smile and let her dip into the bucket with a beaker. The milk looked creamy and smelt of grass.

The boys drank it eagerly, taking turns from the beaker their mother held. Medi was hopeful. If the boys didn't have too much sweet stuff, they might stay healthy – for some time, but the mother was trying to give them honey. Davey was trying to explain to the boys that it was bad for them, but it was hard. After a bit though, they seemed to catch on, and started to nod in understanding. Ari said that they'd gorged themselves on honeycomb the day before. They'd found a bees' nest, and eaten from it before they told their mother and father. So that's what had brought on the coma! They thought they'd been ill because they'd offended the gods, by flouting the Law of Food Sharing, which said you must always tell the rest of the tribe if you found food, not eat it first.

Davey was fascinated by everything they said, everything he saw, but Medi was getting anxious. The sun was directly above the chimney hole now. It must be noon. She wanted to get back to the mound – now. It had been noon twentieth-century time when she'd activated the doors in KwikMart and found herself at the entrance to the circle. Noon, that was surely a good time to try?

'Come on, Davey.' He was eating some of their blaanda bread now. She shook his arm. 'We've got to go.' She could see the mound through the doorway. There were people on it.

He said, 'Not yet, Medi. We must just make sure that Keira is all right.' It was one excuse after another.

But he did join her in the doorway – while Ari and Dev changed into the new clothes Kara had made them for the Gathering Feast – breeches like their father's. They had to wash and oil their bodies before they put them on.

Outside everyone seemed busy, washing, putting on

new clothes or preparing food. The air was filled with the fresh smell of mint and thyme. Outside the hut next door one woman was chopping herbs and another was pummelling them into a piece of dough. Further along a group of women were combing each other's hair with wooden combs, plaiting and weaving the long strands and threading them with corn and flowers. It was as if they were getting ready for a party.

The Corn Priest, with his magnificent head-dress and his cloak of straw, was moving from group to group, talking to people. Most seemed pleased to see him. Only the arrowmaker snubbed him. He didn't even look up, didn't stop chipping for a moment, but when a group of men came by – on their way to the mound – carrying antlers over their shoulders, he muttered something about digging it deep.

So that's what the sawn-off antlers were for – digging the grave. The antlers did look like pick-axes. The men said they would dig deep enough to bury the Corn Maiden, and the arrowmaker spat on the ground. The men repeated that they would dig a grave deep enough for the Corn Maiden, so that she could lie in the ground then rise again in the spring. The arrowmaker spat again and said they would see. What would they see?

Medi wondered how the search party was getting on. There was no sign of them returning with or without Keira. Would the Corn Priest be able to keep the people on his side? Would they celebrate the Gathering Feast in the new way or the old? She wanted to get Davey home before the contest – if there was one – began.

More and more people were arriving – from surrounding settlements it seemed. Corn People greeted River People and River People greeted Forest People. Excitement mounted as family welcomed family. Young men and women looked at each other shyly, and some not so shyly, for the Gathering Feast was also a time of choosing it seemed, a time when partners were chosen for weddings at Leaf Fall.

But the sun was beginning to move across the sky. It wouldn't be midday for much longer. They had to get up the mound – quickly. They had to find their exit. She pulled Davey's arm roughly and didn't let go.

'We've got to go – now!'

Chapter 14

They saw the Corn Maiden as they passed the priest's house on the way to the mound. It was propped against the wall and a man on a ladder was putting a garland of poppies and cornflowers round her neck. Someone else was repairing a damaged bit. Davey wanted to stop and watch. Medi wouldn't let him.

All around them people were talking about the coming feast, and the rights and wrongs of the New Way. Not that it was so new – no one remembered the last human sacrifice. Only the very old remembered their fathers telling them about it. Some told stories of an even earlier time when the chief himself had been sacrificed – every seven years. They had worshipped different gods then.

Now they sacrificed to the Earth Mother. Death for life and life for death, that was the way of things, but they killed a ram, so that Earth Mother would send new lambs in the spring, and they buried the Corn Maiden so that Earth Mother would send new corn.

Most people preferred the New Way. A few said it was dangerous to defy Crowman.

Medi hurried Davey on, she didn't want him to hear the dissident voices. She asked him what he'd been doing since she'd seen him last. He said that when he'd arrived on the mound, he'd seen Ari and Dev in the cornfield next to it. It was evening. They'd been sent to scare the birds away. Then they'd seen him – and he'd joined in chasing the birds away – till the birds had gone to roost. Then they'd taken him home and hidden him in the roof-space. It was where they stored food and extra animal skins for winter. The boys had brought him more food, then he'd gone to sleep – under a wolfskin! He wanted to go back to the boys. He really liked them, he said.

Medi said, 'Don't you want to go home?'

He didn't answer. It was as if he'd forgotten about his previous life. She recognised the feeling and knew that she would have to remember for both of them.

She pointed to the circle of totems on the mound, in front of them now. They were climbing a path up to it. 'Let's see what's happening up there.'

There was plenty happening on either side of them. It reminded her of a picnic day on the school playing fields. Some people were eating – they had blaanda and eggs and blackberries and fish. Some of them were cooking over small fires – they'd brought the blackened hearthstones from their houses with them – and they were boiling eggs by dropping hot stones into a pot of water, and roasting fish on sticks. One man was actually lighting a fire – rubbing sticks together between the palms of his hands – till a wisp of smoke and then a flame appeared.

Medi almost dragged Davey up the path that led to the entrance of the circle. She could see the gateway clearly now, see the gateposts shining in the sun. Which one was the magical one? What must she do to make the magic work? The gate was open. There was a man crouched by it.

Soon they could see that he was painting one of the posts. Higher up, more men seemed to be painting the totems in the inner circle. Others were feeding the fires round the roasting sheep, or adding branches to unlit piles round the central totem, whose antlers glistened red in the sunshine – and just visible to one side of it, was the digging party.

They could see the earth flying, hear snatches of song as the men swung their antler axes.

'Swing low. Swing high.

Earth Mother, all things die.'

There were four men hacking at the earth, and another four moving it out of the way with shovels made of shoulder blades. They moved rhythmically. It was like a dance. And the earth piled up behind them.

Clearly they were digging the grave for Corn Maiden – or Keira.

She glanced back at the settlement – and saw the search party returning.

Was Keira with them? She thought not. Didn't want to know. Didn't want Davey to know.

Now they were standing by the entrance at the painter's elbow, and he, unaware of them, was putting the finishing touch to a crow's round eye. Medi wanted to push him aside and grasp the post. She wanted to push it hard – just as she'd pushed the glass doors of KwikMart. And she still wanted to. Had to.

But Davey was pulling her arm now and pointing down the slope towards the settlement. For a moment she thought he had seen the returning search party.

But it was something else. A roll of drums focused her gaze – on four men hoisting the Corn Maiden onto their shoulders, turning now to face the mound. And the Corn Priest was stepping in front of them, and a crowd was forming itself into a crocodile behind the Corn Maiden, and as Medi and Davey and the painter and everyone else on the mound watched, a procession began to move off – to the lively beat of a drum.

And people were still hurrying to join the procession. Below them the picnic-makers were making their way down the slope, and now the people above them, the painters and diggers and the fire-pile builder, were filing through the exit, being careful not to smudge the wet gateposts.

Then the painter himself gave the crow a last flick of black paint, and picked up his paints. Then he followed the others, running to catch them up.

Medi saw her chance, but knew she would have to be quick.

Unfortunately Davey had moved out of her reach. He was watching the procession which was now moving away from the settlement – with people still rushing to join it and he looked as if *he* wanted to join it. It was heading east towards the forest.

'Come on!' She grabbed his hand. 'We've got to go home, Davey!'

He pulled away from her and said he thought he could

see Ari and Dev.

She said, 'I'm going even if you're not!' She was lying of course, and perhaps he knew, or didn't care, because he still didn't come.

So she went and knelt down in front of him, so that she was looking straight into his eyes and she said, 'Davey, listen to me.' Then she explained very clearly what had happened and what she was going to do. What *they* were going to do. What they *had* to do.

She said, 'Trust me, Davey.'

He walked to the entrance with her. Then they stood together facing the gatepost on the left-hand side. Davey stood in front of Medi, so that her arms were round him, her hands on either side of his.

Praying, she said, 'Push, Davey!' – and with their hands on the sticky post, they pushed.

Chapter 15

Nothing happened.

Medi pushed till she hurt, but nothing happened. Davey gave up much sooner. Afterwards he turned round to look at her, holding up his hands as if he expected her to get a tissue and wipe them. They were red. She looked at her own covered in yellow.

'And we've spoilt the man's painting.' He looked accusing.

She felt foolish and desperate. How were they going to get home? Were they trapped here for ever? She thought she was going to be sick. Her throat was sore, her stomach heaved and she could feel her pulses pounding.

Davey wiped his hands on the grass. Medi wiped hers down her skirt. When she could speak she said, 'We'll try again later.'

Davey didn't answer. He was watching the procession now wending its way along the far side of a field skirting the forest. It was heading for the river. You could see the Corn Maiden and identify the Priest but it was too far away to see other individuals. Davey was looking for Ari and Dev. He said so. He was worried about them, and he liked being with their family. He certainly wasn't in a hurry to return to his own.

They both watched for a while and they saw the Priest stop – because he'd reached the river bank. You could see the surface of the water gleaming, as sunrays slanted down from the western sky. Medi could feel them, warm on her cheek. It was well past midday. How *were* they going to get home?

Slowly – everything seemed to be happening so slowly – the procession changed direction. It started to move towards them, following the line of the winding river. Medi wondered if they were walking the bounds – she'd heard of a ceremony like that. Occasionally the Priest's voice reached them, praising the Earth Mother, assuring her of their thanks.

'We give to you, that you may give to us.'

And the followers chanted in reply, 'And you give to us, that we may give to you.'

Sometimes there was singing, and always there was the drum – like a heartbeat, there when you listened for it, there when you didn't. Pa-rum. Pa-rum.

Were they trapped here for ever?

Pa-rum. Pa-rum.

Davey watched in silence. Medi tried to speak to him, tried to explain about the importance of getting home, but her words made no impression. How could she convince him that they must try again? She was determined to get them home, whether Davey wanted to or not. But how? What else could she do? It would be harder getting Davey to co-operate next time. He seemed tired now. She felt tired too. She sat down beside him, and he put his head in her lap.

They must both have fallen asleep – and slept for quite

a while – because when she next looked the procession was back at the settlement. She felt colder too. As she watched, the Priest turned to face the mound and seemed to be examining the sky, the western sky where the banked clouds were fiery red. So sunset couldn't be far off. *Sunset!*

As the word came into her head, Medi looked around to see if Crowman and Keira were anywhere about, but couldn't see them among the crowd. Then she looked towards the forest, which resounded with the clamour of bird cries. Crows wheeled in the sky above the forest edge, but there was no sign of Crowman, no sign of his prisoner either. Where were they?

Para-rum para-rum. As the drumbeat quickened, the Corn Priest began to climb the hill. He was moving towards her at quite a pace, and so were the people behind him. In single file now, it was hard to believe they'd been walking for hours, they were walking so fast. And the Corn Maiden's bearers still held her high above their heads.

Para-rum! Para-rara-rum-ra! As they got closer Medi saw that the people in the procession were linked now. Each with their hands on the shoulders of the person in front, they were *shimmying* their way up the slope. Even the Corn Maiden's bearers had a spring in their steps.

Para-rara-rum-ra! Para-rara-rum-ra!

It was as if a snake was twisting and writhing its way up the winding path. Then the snake stopped suddenly, and the Priest's voice rang out.

'As the sun sets and rises again,

So from death comes life again.'

Rattles and drums kept time with his words.

And the people-snake repeated his words. 'So from death comes life again.'

Then the people-snake danced again – and stopped again.

And the Priest's voice rang out again.

'As the elk's antlers grow anew,
So life grows anew.'

'Out of death comes life!' The people-snake's voice was loud and clear!

'As the serpent's skin grows anew,
So life grows anew.'

'Out of death comes life!' So it went on till the Priest was standing in front of the entrance. Medi could have touched his golden cloak. 'We thank you, Earth Mother. Accept our gifts.'

He raised both hands, one holding the sacred staff – now she could see a corn serpent coiled round it – then he carried on walking, through the gate, up to the mound.

Entranced, Medi didn't notice Davey waking up, as the procession passed by her. The young women looked so lovely with their braided hair intertwined with buttercups and daisies, and their new deerskin tunics. The young men's bare torsos shone as if they'd been polished with oil.

'I didn't see Ari or Dev, Medi.'

She jumped when Davey spoke. The procession, halfway up the mound now, had stopped. The Corn

Priest was standing by one of the totems in the upper circle, and as she watched the snake started to dance again – weaving in and out of the totems. Medi said she thought she had seen Ari and Dev with their parents, near the front of the procession. She thought they must have passed by before Davey woke up.

He said, 'Was Keira with them?'

She said, 'No.'

But she was less worried about Keira now. The Gathering Feast was underway – that was clear – with the Corn Priest in charge, and they were celebrating in the New Way. They were going to sacrifice the Corn Maiden. Her grave was waiting at the top of the mound. Everyone seemed happy with things as they were. Any second now the sun would drop below the horizon. By the time Crowman and Keira arrived the Corn Maiden would be beneath the earth. It would be too late to sacrifice Keira.

She would like to have seen her before they went, but she wasn't going to wait beyond sunset. She wasn't going to wait for anyone. At sunset she was going to try again. Sunset. That must be a good time to try.

Not long now – the sun was a smouldering fire just visible through smoke-grey cloud.

She glanced towards the woods – still no sign of Keira or Crowman. Closer to, though, she could see someone else, also watching the woods. It was the young man, Keira's admirer. He was crouched behind a bush, a bow at his side.

Then a new sound, of lilting pipes, distracted her for

a moment, to the top of the mound where young women were dancing – it looked like a maypole dance – round the central totem. She said, 'Look, Davey.'

But he was watching the young man whose bow was drawn back now – and Medi saw why. Keira and Crowman had suddenly appeared. Clearly the young man was taking no chances. He had them in his sights. Crowman was urging Keira to walk faster, but she was stumbling, her hands behind her back. They were coming straight up the slope, ignoring the path, heading straight for the entrance to the mound.

The young man adjusted his position. He was waiting – Medi could see that – till Crowman was level with him. Then he was going to shoot.

He was taking aim now – as two men rushed out from some nearby bushes. Overpowering him, they dragged him to one side as Medi pushed Davey onto the grass. Then they both lay flat, hoping that Crowman hadn't seen them.

The hideous figure passed by them, Keira stumbling in front of him.

Her face was red – at first Medi thought she had been crying – maybe she had – but the red on her face was red earth. Her hands were smeared with it too. Her wrists were bound by a leather thong. Crowman held it. They passed through the gate.

The news travelled. The word went round. 'The shaman. He's coming. Crowman, he's here.'

'Keira has the mark of death upon her.' Was that what the red smears were?

The rhythm of the drums faltered, the dancers paused. And the Corn Priest commanded, 'Play on! Dance on! We shall celebrate in the New Way!' And the players played and the dancers danced as the Crowman and Keira climbed the mound.

In the west the blood-red sun was sinking.

Crowman urged Keira to hurry. The young man struggled against his captors.

The blood-red sun was sinking fast.

Medi turned to Davey, 'Come on, we must . . .' *But Davey wasn't there.*

'Stop, old man!' The Corn Priest stood in front of Crowman, who had reached the second circle of totems. Crowman pushed him aside. Then he scrambled ahead of Keira, yanking the thong that bound her wrists. She spun round so that for a moment Medi saw her anguished face. *Where was Davey?* Keira was flat on her face now, and Crowman was dragging her up the slope.

The music and dancing had stopped. Now all eyes were on Crowman and Keira whom he held against his chest, her throat outstretched. In Crowman's right hand was a knife.

The Corn Priest roared, 'Stop, Crowman! Release the girl!'

And Medi saw Davey standing behind Crowman.

She began a frantic scramble up the slope with Crowman's voice in her ears. 'As the sun sinks, the maid must die!'

His hand came down.

And Davey rushed forward knocking the knife from his hands.

Then Dal and Kara grabbed Keira and pulled her to one side.

And Medi – wondering why her legs were moving in slow motion – saw Crowman whirling round. Saw his arm round Davey's neck. Saw his other hand holding up Davey's paint-smeared hand.

'Desecrater of the sacred totems!' His voice was a high-pitched wail. 'The gods will have blood!'

'Earth Mother has the blood of seven rams!' The Corn Priest pointed to their carcasses on spits round the fire. 'Go home, old man. Come.' He set off towards the grave. Clearly he thought the danger was over, couldn't *see* Davey. The people followed him.

'Give me the maid!' Crowman screeched.

'Give me the boy! Earth Mother orders you!' Medi, reaching the top at last, made her breathless voice as powerful as she could, but Crowman kept hold of Davey. No one came forward to help her.

Surely Ari and Dev and Keira could see Davey? But they were hugging each other, weren't even looking this way.

Davey looked terrified, but at least Crowman didn't have the knife.

'Give me the boy!' Medi took a step forward, but Crowman kept his arm round Davey's neck.

'Get back, witch!' Crowman could see her – that was clear. She must make him release Davey.

'The gods forbid human sacrifice!'

'The gods give life. The gods take life!' Crowman's hand moved closer to Davey's neck, and Medi saw something in his hand, wriggling. She saw a *snake's* tongue flicking in and out. Desperate, she reached into her pocket. He thought she was Crow Maiden did he, a being with supernatural powers?

Well then. 'Cawk! Cawk!' She flapped her fringed arms.

'Cawk!' She made sure he saw the hand mirror she was holding. Made sure he saw his reflection.

'Crow Maiden gives life. And . . .' She turned the mirror in her hand so that his reflection disappeared. 'Crow Maiden takes life.'

Crowman stepped back, then he leaned forward – mesmerised. He had seen his reflection before, fleetingly, in the river sometimes, but he had never seen it so clearly. And he had never seen it appear and disappear at someone's bidding. This Crow Maiden did powerful magic.

But he still had his arm round Davey's neck. He still had the snake in his other hand.

'Crow Maiden gives life.' She repeated the action. 'And she takes life. So let my brother go, old man.'

He didn't move.

So Medi moved. She reached forward and grasped his horny beak. The mask came off in her hand and the face before her crumpled. And a white-haired old *woman* stood before her.

Medi said, 'I have your soul, lady. Release my brother, or I will destroy it.'

Davey shot to her side.

Still Medi held out the mirror. 'I have your soul in my power, old woman. Go away and never return or I will destroy it.'

Now a powerful voice boomed from the top of the mound. 'Earth Mother is ready to receive Corn Maiden!'

They could see the silhouette of the Corn Priest on top of the mound, and of the crowd gathering round the grave.

Again the Corn Priest's voice rang out, 'Let the celebrations begin!'

There was a roll of drums and a skirl of pipes. The sun was a scarlet thread on the blue-black horizon.

As the old woman seemed to shrink into the shadows, Medi took Davey's hand. 'Come on,' she said. 'There isn't much time. We've got to try and get home.'

Chapter 16

As she stood in the entrance for the second time that day, Medi felt horribly afraid. What if it didn't work this time? She glanced at the post on her left, the one they had pushed earlier. They had spoiled the paintwork, that was all. A crow's smudged face looked at her accusingly. She was going to try the other one this time and push in the opposite direction.

'What if we try widdershins, Davey? What if we push the other way?'

He looked at her blankly, then turned back to the action on the mound, where the dancers were spinning and leaping round the smouldering fires. Hands linked, they whirled first one way then the other, and drummers crouched round them, beating time with the flats of their hands.

Pararum pararum para-rara-rum!

The beat quickened, and a sound like the wind in the trees curled round the beats, as pipers got to their feet and raised their pipes to greet the moon, which now appeared from behind a cloud – first a sliver, then a slice and then a whole orange moon, which the dancers greeted with wild cries and higher leaps!

It was a sight she would never forget.

'Put your hands here, Davey.' She had to take hold of him, turn him to face the post, place his hands on either side of it. Then she stood behind him, her hands either side of his.

'Push!'

Nothing happened.

'Push!' She tried again but Davey didn't.

The drums went quiet. Everything went quiet as the moon went behind a cloud. It was the same quiet that she'd noticed when she arrived. She could feel it flowing round her.

Then came another sound, from the top of the mound. A low murmur became a hum, which became a rhythmic chant.

'No time
No place
Nowhere
No face
No who
No why. Earth Mother, all things die.'

It was very dark. The fires had burned low. The moon stayed behind the cloud. Then the chorus of voices began again.

'No time
No place
Nowhere
No face
No who
No why.
Earth Mother, all things die.'

The voices were low, downbeat, resigned – and they filled Medi with sadness. She could just see Davey's face in the darkness. He looked sad too.

Silence. Emptiness. Nothingness – was that all there was?

No, there was something else. As the moon appeared from behind a cloud, there was a stirring on top of the mound, and a voice broke the silence, followed by another voice, and another, each voice coming from a different direction.

'I am the moon!

I am the sky!

I am the earth!

I am the fire!'

These voices were clear, upbeat, and growing in confidence.

'I am the rushing river!

I am the raven on the rock!

I am the salmon in the sea!

I am the seed in the earth!

I am the wind in the trees!

I am a courageous bull!'

The voices grew louder.

'I am a powerful giant!

I can shift my shape like a god!'

Hearing them, Medi felt an overwhelming urge to join her voice to theirs and grabbing Davey she called out, 'I am a strong-necked swan!'

And placing both his hands on the totem, she yelled at the top of her voice. *'Idemedi! Yevadavey! Idemedi! Yevadavey!'*

And she felt the post give way . . .

It was still raining. The rain was bouncing off the tarmac and the entrance was thick with crows clamouring to shelter under the canopy. The revolving doors had broken down again. Medi and Davey were stuck inside. In the car park a red-coated supervisor was trying to shoo the birds away. Davey laughed. The supervisor stared at him through the glass. She scrutinised his face. Then she went to read a billboard outside the store:

A boy disappeared
from this store at approximately 7pm
Wednesday 24th July
Anyone remembering seeing him should
contact the police immediately.

There was a photograph of Davey.

Medi and Davey looked at each other. Then Medi looked at her watch which said 1 o'clock. So she'd been missing for only an hour. Amazing. Davey nudged her and pointed to a police enquiry desk just inside the store. There was a policeman sitting behind it. Another supervisor was talking to him. They both kept glancing at Medi and Davey. Davey waved at them. Then the doors started to move – and she felt assaulted by sound. The air seemed to throb with whirring – and clapping!

'Out of the time-machine, Medi!' Davey laughed as he stepped into the store and ran towards the police desk.

Medi turned towards the sound of clapping which was

coming from the car park – where Mrs Merridew, with a towel round her head, was standing with Mrs Vogel and a lot of other middle-aged ladies and a few men, all holding hands in what seemed to be a circle going right round the store. They all had corn dollies pinned to their chests.

Mrs Merridew clapped again. 'It worked! It worked! Davey has returned! You can open your eyes now!'

She had Gulliver with her in a wicker cage.

Behind her, a line of very wet, but otherwise remarkably ordinary-looking men and women opened their eyes.

'See! Mind over matter!' cried Mrs Vogel. There was a dead crow at her feet.

'Oh dear,' she said. 'Someone must have run into it. I can't do anything for that one, I'm afraid. Medi! How nice to see you!'

Then a policeman took Medi's arm. It was PC Lawless. 'Where have you been for the past hour?' he said. 'And where did you find the little boy?'

'What was that you said?' Davey asked a few days later when they were talking about it again. They were on the top of a double decker bus. 'When you pushed that totem, what did you say?'

'Idemedi,' said Medi, 'and Yevadavey.'

Joe-boy laughed. 'Is that another language, Medi?'

Davey said, 'Tell me. What's it mean?'

Medi said, 'Think about it. It came to me in a dream.'

The three of them were on their way to St Mark's

church on the other side of the town. They could see its grey tower from the bridge near the market square. It was an old disused church. Well, it wasn't used as a church any more, it was used by the county council's archaeology department.

When they got there – and eventually found a way in – Medi told a Mrs Butler that they wanted to know about the prehistoric settlement at KwikMart. Mrs Butler, who was neat and grey and smaller than Medi, said she specialised in statuary and she looked a bit like a statue herself. She stood very still and she held her hands in a praying position. Medi said they wanted to know about the skeletons that they'd found there, of the children, the prehistoric children.

Davey said, 'Show her the leaflet, Medi' – because Mrs Butler looked as if she didn't know what Medi was talking about. So Medi showed her the leaflet with the drawing of the skeletons on the front. She said they really wanted to see the skeletons.

Mrs Butler looked thoughtful while she read it. Then she said she would see what she could do and went off to another part of the building. She said they could have a look round if they liked.

The church still looked like a church. It had enormous pillars and stained glass windows, but it also looked like a builders' yard. There were piles of wood and bricks all over the place and lots of boxes. They could hear someone scraping something in another part of the building. Then the scraping stopped and they could hear Mrs Butler talking to someone. They listened but they couldn't hear what she was saying.

Davey said, 'Do you think we saved them, Medi? Do you think we saved Ari and Dev and Keira?'

Joe-boy said, "Course you did. Tell me again, Davey.' He thought it was a brill story and didn't mind how many times Davey told him it.

Medi said, 'I don't know, Davey.' Then she said, 'We saved them once.' She really didn't know. That's why they'd come. If they could see the skeletons they'd have more information. She wanted to see the size of the skeletons. She wished she was a pathologist. She wanted to examine them.

Davey said, 'It's nice about Mum and Frank, isn't it?'

Medi said, 'Yes. Very nice.' She was sure about that. Her mother and father were trying to 'get it together again' – their words. They had been trying for a while it seemed. Frank had visited once or twice, so Medi had been right when she thought she'd smelt his aftershave that day, and Jenny had gone to meet him the night Davey disappeared, when she said she'd gone to work. They'd met on several occasions. Jenny hadn't told her because she didn't want to raise her hopes. She still didn't want to raise her hopes. She'd said, 'You can't turn back the clock, Medi.'

'But it's not so good about Des,' said Davey.

'No.'

It had been hard for Davey – and Joe-boy – learning that their dad was in prison. But at least Davey had been able to prove that he hadn't been fibbing when he said he'd seen his dad. He had seen him through the window of the Community Centre, and he'd thought he had come for him – which he had in a sense, he'd wanted to see his son – but when Davey got outside Des had gone. He'd taken fright, when he'd seen Davey go and tell Mrs Bentley. So he hadn't been there when Davey went outside to meet him. That's when Davey had decided to go and find Medi and Joe-boy and get his leaf.

'What then? What happened when you got to KwikMart?' asked Medi.

'I saw Ari and Dev through the glass, though I didn't know they were Ari and Dev then,' he said. 'And I wanted to know about them. I'd wanted to know about them for a long time. You wouldn't tell me anything.'

'I didn't know anything.'

'You wouldn't even talk about it. You thought it would scare me.'

She couldn't deny that.

'Anyway, one minute I was longing to know all about them, and the next minute I was there. I tripped I think.' There was still a bit of a bruise on his head where he'd hit the door.

He had told everyone what had happened. So had Medi – though not in such vivid detail as Davey. She didn't expect people to believe her. They believed the bit about Davey bumping his head and they thought his *visions*, as they called them, were the result of concussion. They thought that an electric shock might have caused him – and Medi – to fall. So they had changed the faulty doors.

Mrs Butler came back with a very hairy man in a red plaid shirt. He said his name was Danny and he was very apologetic. He said they couldn't see the skeletons because he couldn't find them. They weren't where he thought they were. They had been catalogued and put in store, he was sure of that, but the archaeologist in charge of that project had left because funds had been withdrawn. He even wondered if she'd taken them with her.

Mrs Butler said they needed to have a really good tidy up, but they were too short-staffed at the moment. Danny asked Medi if they could come back some other day, and perhaps give them notice beforehand, so someone could have a good look before they arrived.

Medi promised that she would. She was very disappointed, felt cheated somehow, but Davey wasn't even upset. In fact he seemed ecstatically happy. Going home on the bus, he had his arm round Joe-boy and such a big smile on his face that his mouth nearly reached his ears. Medi thought that it was because he'd had a letter from his dad that day. Des was back in prison; he'd given himself up as soon as he'd heard that Davey was missing. Jenny said Des wasn't all bad – just too easily led by greedier people.

But when Medi said, 'What are you smiling about, Davey?' he said, 'We did it, Medi. We saved them. They didn't die, not when they were little anyway.' He thought the skeletons had vanished – into thin air – and that's why the archaeologists couldn't find them.

She didn't say anything, she couldn't. She didn't

know, but she doubted it somehow. Let Davey believe what made him happy. Now he was telling Joe-boy how he had played ball with Ari and Dev – with a stone ball!

Looking down at the plump pigeons in the market square, Medi saw Sarah with Harvey and Gray Parker and she waved, but they didn't see her. Never mind, she was seeing them tonight. They were all going to a film. Jenny was babysitting – or boy-sitting – as the boys preferred to call it!

Medi smiled at her reflection in the window pane.

What had Jenny said? You can't turn the clock back?

Maybe you couldn't. She'd make up her own mind about that later. Right now she was more than happy to let time move forward.

Order Form

To order direct from the publishers, just make a list of the titles you want and fill in the form below:

Name

....

Address

....

....

....

Send to: Dept 6, HarperCollins Publishers Ltd, Westerhill Road, Bishopbriggs, Glasgow G64 2QT.

Please enclose a cheque or postal order to the value of the cover price, plus:

UK & BFPO: Add £1.00 for the first book, and 25p per copy for each additional book ordered.

Overseas and Eire: Add £2.95 service charge. Books will be sent by surface mail but quotes for airmail despatch will be given on request.

A 24-hour telephone ordering service is available to holders of Visa, MasterCard, Amex or Switch cards on 0141-772 2281.

Collins
An *Imprint of* HarperCollins*Publishers*